The Boss and the Wedding Mess

Adora Prince

Adora Prince

1st Edition 2025

Cover Design: Luv & Lee Publishing

Editing: Luv & Lee Publishing

All rights reserved. Reproduction, even in part, is prohibited. No part of this work may be reproduced, duplicated, or distributed in any form without the written permission of the author. This book is a work of fiction. All events and characters described in this book are fictional. Any resemblance to real persons, living or deceased, is purely coincidental and unintentional.

This book contains explicit scenes and is not suitable for readers under the age of 18.

LUV & LEE PUBLISHING LLC
3833 Powerline Road Suite 101
Fort Lauderdale, FL. US33309

Contents

Prologue	1
Chapter 1	5
Chapter 2	10
Chapter 3	15
Chapter 4	18
Chapter 5	20
Chapter 6	25
Chapter 7	32
Chapter 8	41
Chapter 9	44
Chapter 10	51
Chapter 11	56
Chapter 12	64
Chapter 13	68
Chapter 14	78
Chapter 15	86
Chapter 16	94
Chapter 17	99
Chapter 18	108
Chapter 19	112

Chapter 20	118
Chapter 21	123
Chapter 22	128
Chapter 23	130
Chapter 24	141
Chapter 25	143
Chapter 26	154
Chapter 27	160
Chapter 28	164
Chapter 29	168
Chapter 30	176
Chapter 31	179
Thank you	185

Prologue

London

I stared at my best friend sternly. It's so stern that she finally comes clean after I've been trying to get her to open up in the car for almost an hour.

"It's the *St Mary the Virgin, Mortlake*."

She hangs her head, and her blonde curls fall partially across her face, hiding her flushed cheeks and tear-stained eyes.

"Okay." I turn the key in my car's ignition, start the engine, and give her a determined look. Then I tie my long dark hair up in a ponytail and drive off. "We can still make it in time!"

She's previously admitted that this unfaithful jerk's wedding is taking place at exactly 3 PM, so we still have a whole twenty minutes to warn his fiancée about this creep. She absolutely must not marry him!

"Not so fast," Vanessa gasps nervously, holding onto the grip above the passenger door while I floor it and race down the main road.

"If you'd just come clean right away and told me which church they're getting married in, I could drive slower now."

At least the roads aren't so crowded, even though it's Saturday, allowing us to make good progress.

"I just don't want us to crash," she stammers, clutching her bag with her other hand. A lipstick flies out when I have to take a curve and we're both pushed to the side like we're on a roller coaster. "London!"

"Just let me handle this," I answer confidently. "It's fate that you just found out he's getting married today, and it's fate you told me about it. Whatever planet's responsible for this, it wants us to stop this wedding!"

"I don't even want him back," she says with a sob.

"Us women have to stick together! A man like that should never be allowed to marry. He'll cheat on her too. Just imagine what she'll go through when she finds out who's really her husband when it's too late? I would want someone to tell me the truth. Wouldn't you?"

"Yes, I suppose..."

"There you go." We're coming up at a traffic light. Just as I hit the gas, it flips.

"London? Hey! The light's red. Red! Bright red!" Vanessa yells, staring at me in shock as I fly through the intersection.

"It was still yellow."

"No, it was already red!"

"Dark yellow. Orange at most."

"Oh, London..." Vanessa looks like she's about to have a heart attack, so I ease off the gas a little.

She's not totally wrong. Safety first. But I'm furious. When Vanessa found out her boyfriend was getting married today—and that she'd only ever been the mistress—her whole world fell apart. I can't even imagine how much she's suffering right now.

Good thing I know this church. A friend of ours got married here two years ago, but that marriage is on solid foundations and they're still happy to this day, at least from the outside. But really, you never know what goes on behind closed doors.

It's 2:57. We have three minutes left. I'm a little out of breath and my cheeks are burning.

"Do you really want to go in there?" Vanessa asks nervously, staring out the window. There are at least fifty cars in the parking lot. The doors are already closed, and organ music is spilling all the way out to the street.

Okay, now that I'm here, my courage briefly wavers. In my head, I pictured myself storming right in without hesitation.

"I have to. Nobody treats my best friend like that. Nobody gets to break your heart the way he did."

"Oh London..." I manage to coax a small smile from her. I quickly unbuckle and lean over to Vanessa so I can hug her. "You're such a fighter. I'm really grateful that you're here for me..."

"Through thick and thin. We promised." I pull back and hook my pinky with hers. "And now I'm going to kick that guy where the sun don't shine."

I leave the key in the ignition and step out of my little red speedster—Tomato, as I call her. My face is nearly the same shade. With purpose, I slam the door shut and head toward the church. It's old, and the walls yellowed with age, but the path is lined with white roses as I walk past. They really went all out, I have to admit.

With each step I take toward the church door, I'm getting queasier. But I have to do this. For Vanessa. And for the poor woman who's about to make the biggest mistake of her life.

I reach the dark brown doors, grab the handle and take one more deep breath, before I push it open. The organ music hits my ears, and to my shock, the bride and groom are already standing at the altar, gazing at each other. Oh no! What's going on? This wasn't supposed to have started yet.

The church is packed all the way to the back rows, and several of the well-dressed guests turn to look at me as I enter.

Have they already said, "*I do*"?

Doesn't matter. It's now or never!

"Stop! I have something to say!" I shout, startled by how incredibly loudly my voice echoes in the church.

Now *everyone* turns to look at me, like in a really bad movie.

And I mean, everyone!

The stunning bride stunning in a long veil, over her brown curls. The absolute ass of a groom is in his cream-colored suit and greasy gelled hair. The bridesmaids in light blue, and the groomsmen on the other side, in cream, matching the groom. Even the pastor pauses to adjust his glasses while everyone's staring at me.

Now or never, London. You've come this far. Don't give up!

Murmurs begin an older gentleman beside me snaps, "How dare you barge in here and..."

"This man is a cheater!" I shout, jabbing a freshly manicured pastel pink finger at the groom. "Don't marry him! He had an affair with my best friend."

Guests gasp. The bride stares at the jerk in horror, while the rest exchange irritated looks.

"My best friend thought she was the only one, until she found out today that she was just the mistress while her boyfriend was getting married! How can anyone be that cruel?" Then I look straight at the bride, dropping my arm. "Run, sister. Don't waste your life on this idiot."

""Is that true, Marc?" she cries, devastated.

Marc? Wait—Marc?

I go quiet. Shit. I need to think. Something is wrong.

"What is this nonsense?" one of the groomsmen snaps, rushing toward me, while the so-called Marc tries to comfort his bride. She doesn't seem thrilled at all about the bitter truth.

"Is the groom's name Marc?" I ask the older gentleman next to me.

"Yes. Marc Brown," he confirms angrily.

"Not Dominic?"

"No. His name is Marc. As I said. Marc. Not Dominic."

As I stand there petrified, the groomsman is charging at me, and his look says it all: he's not particularly happy that I'm here.

"Explain this to me, Marc!" the bride demands, agitated.

"Stephanie, I have no idea what she's talking about!" he protests.

Oh God. Her name's Stephanie?

"Fuck, I'm in the wrong church," I blurt out in panic.

The older gentleman next to me can't believe it. "Is this some kind of joke?"

The dark-haired groomsman is almost on top of me, so I bolt. I'm only wearing laced sandals and a knee-length pleated skirt, but they're still good for running.

"Sorry! I'm in the wrong church!" I call out before pulling the door open again and squeezing through the narrow gap. I step outside and run as fast as I can to my car. "Buckle up, we need to go!"

"Hey! Stop right there!" the guy behind me shouts furiously, nearly ripping the church door off its hinges.

Damn it. I have to hurry.

I reach the car, open the door, and see the guy rushing toward me like a steam engine. I immediately get in, lock the door, and fire up the engine.

"What's going on? Who is that?" Vanessa asks me, confused, while the guy reaches the driver's door and tries to open it.

"Hey, open up!" He slaps the glass—not hard, just enough to get my attention. No chance.

"This is the wrong church!" I say and glance at Vanessa, who looks unsurprised. "Seriously?"

She must not have wanted to tell me the right church, so we'd be late. "Oh, come on, I crashed the wrong wedding!"

"Okay, yes... I'm sorry!" Vanessa admits.

"What was that about?" the guy outside shouts. I continue to ignore him until I finally gather my courage, take a deep breath and finally crack the window an inch so he can hear me clearly.

"Hi, yes, sorry. Wrong church. Thanks for your understanding."

"Excuse me? Understanding?" he asks incredulously and takes a step back as I floor the gas and speed off with squealing tires.

I can still see him standing in the rearview mirror with his arms spread wide. I'm so mortified I wish I could sink through the floor. Thankfully, I'll never see him or this wedding party ever again...

Chapter 1

London

I stop a few streets away and take a deep breath, turn off the engine, and look at Vanessa.

"I assume you don't want to tell me which is the right church?"

"Are you thinking of going there now too?" she asks, her voice trembling so much I almost start crying myself.

"No, it's okay." I take my hands off the steering wheel, rub my face, then reach into the back seat for my purse and grab my water bottle. After a sip, I say, "Those were complete strangers. I hope the bride still marries him. The guy didn't even do anything wrong."

"Maybe we should go back and clear things up?"

"I did shout that I was in the wrong church." Whether that helped... "Better not interfere again."

Vanessa and I sit in silence for a moment.

"Are you mad at me for lying to you?" she asks.

"What? No. No... I put way too much pressure on you. I was so angry at that jerk. I shouldn't have forced you to drive to the church with me to try to stop the wedding." I check the time. It's way too late for that now anyway. "Maybe he's learned from his mistake and will stay faithful to her?" I wish that for her. But I don't believe it.

"How exactly did you find out about it?" There simply wasn't time for this earlier. Between all the tears and my anger, some questions remained unanswered.

"I was in town and met a mutual friend. I asked him what he was doing later, and he told me he was going to a wedding. Then he mentioned names, and I asked to see a photo. There he was. Dominic. It was really my Dominic. What a crazy coincidence."

"It's a small world," I murmur.

"And London's just a village," she adds in a mumble.

Vanessa lowers her gaze, then pulls out her phone. I watch her scroll through photos of them together before deleting them all. "Two months. I never noticed a thing. I mean, we both worked a lot, only saw each other on weekends or talked on the phone in the evenings. How on earth was I supposed to know he had a fiancée?"

"Do you know anything about her?"

"Yes. She has a bakery and is busy on weekends. She even does deliveries herself. Her hours are from 2:00 PM to 8:00 PM. After that, she stays late to prep cake bases. She usually doesn't get home before midnight."

"How do you know all that?" I ask, amazed.

"It's on her blog and Instagram." She shows me the page, where a beaming blonde smiles back. "177,000 followers." She looks again. "177,892... Everyone loves her."

"So that's why he had time for you on weekends and in the evenings. She was occupied with her business. How cruel..."

"Yes," she whispers. "I wanted to marry him. I wanted kids with him. I was so sure." She wipes away a few tears. "We walked through the city, hand in hand. He took me out to dinner, bought me flowers. He never once hinted we might get caught."

"Where's her shop?" I ask.

"Richmond." Southwest London.

"And you live in Romford. That's on the other side of the city. What's the drive? Over an hour?"

"Almost ninety minutes through downtown, about ten less if you take the main roads north."

"So hardly anyone who knew you would've seen you there. Or he just didn't care. He must have felt pretty confident." I take another sip.

"I even went to his place," she sighs. "An apartment just a few streets from mine. It all felt *too* perfect."

"He probably just rented it. That takes a serious amount of scheming." She nods.

"What do you want to do now?"

"Forget him. I've already blocked him everywhere." She looks at me. "Can you drive me home?"

"First, we're getting burgers and ice cream. We both deserve it."

"With extra cheese?"

"Absolutely."

What a miserable Saturday evening. We stuffed ourselves with burgers, fries, and cola. Then we demolished almost three liters of walnut ice cream with whipped cream and washed it down with two bottles of red wine. We eventually passed out on Vanessa's couch, and I didn't make it home until the next day.

Unfortunately, I couldn't find out where that jerk's fake apartment is. I simply have to respect Vanessa's wish not to track him down. I promised, so I'll stick to it, even though it's killing me.

Back in my own apartment, I dig painkillers out of the drawer and swallow them down.

Way too much alcohol last night, but I live for these girls' nights, even when the reason behind them is awful. It's already 4:00 PM. We partied until sunrise, crashing sometime around six or seven. What a crazy night.

"I'm home," I text Vanessa. A heart emoji pops up on my screen. Smiling, I plug in my phone and set it aside. Battery's down to 12%.

I try to be productive, at least a little. Laundry, tidying, chores. That's all I've got in me today. Tomorrow it's back to work, and there's a lot to do. With the company's summer festival coming up, I'll be actively helping out my boss, Arthur Blackthorn. Although he usually handles most things himself, as organizing festive events brings him joy, I'm happy to lend him a hand here and there. He's seventy-six, and while he's still fit for his age and looks younger than he is, occasionally he does need some support. After his surgery and long hospital stay earlier this year he tires more easily. Rumor in the office is he'll soon name a successor, and the vultures are already circling, rubbing hands and sharpening their knives. I'm dreading the day one of them takes over. It's unfortunately only going to make my life in this wonderful company complicated and certainly not easier.

In the evening, I'm only capable of curling up on the couch, enjoying strawberry-vanilla tea, and watching a true crime show. Lately, I've been craving this almost daily.

Unfortunately, I fall asleep on the couch without setting my alarm. When I wake up the next morning, it's already bright out, and I'm lying in probably the most uncomfortable position of my entire life. One leg is half-hanging on the side table, one arm across the cushion, and the other leg bent and dangling over the armrest. My poor back. Maybe you can fall asleep like this at seventeen when you come home from a wild night of partying. At twenty-eight it means I'll need at least a good dose of pain relief cream and a few new bruises that I'll surely wonder where they came from.

Something hard is digging into me.

There's nothing hard here.

Okay, I have found the remote control. It will certainly leave a nice pattern on my back for a while. Fantastic.

Still half-asleep, I reach for my phone and nearly choke. 7:51 AM. I'm supposed to be in the office by 8:30 at the latest.

"Damn it!" I curse and roll onto the floor. Thud!

How am I supposed to shower, get dressed, and drive to work without being late?

Although I've been working for Blackthorn Data Solutions for three years now, I've never been late before, and I'm not breaking my streak today! I strip on the run, leaving a trail of clothes across the living room and down the hall. In the bathroom, I crank on the shower and hop in, taking my toothbrush with me. Whatever. Details don't matter now. I wash myself lightning-fast with minimal effort and run to my bedroom wrapped in a towel.

"Hello bed. Sorry, I cheated on you last night. Won't happen again!"

Then I yank open the closets and dry myself off in front of the full-length mirror.

Well, I look pretty good - except for the remote control pattern on my back. Not good.

Underwear. Bra, nude pantyhose. Then a turquoise blouse, black skirt with a slight drape, and white sneakers. Done. I dash back to the bathroom, put on some deodorant and perfume, my jewelry, and stuff my makeup into a cosmetics bag. I brush my hair, wrap it into a tight bun (but with a small curl at the side of my forehead so I don't look too austere) and leave the bathroom.

I give a last sad look toward the coffee maker. "I'll need you again tomorrow!" I promise, then leave the apartment. And... almost close the door without taking my handbag and keys. Oh, and my phone. I run back inside. It's 8:04. If traffic is merciful, it is twenty minutes to the office. Thirty if the world insists on obeying speed limits.

I stuff everything I have into my bag and run off to the elevator that takes me from the seventh floor to the underground garage. At 8:06, I start the engine and speed off.

Naturally, I hit every red light and take advantage of the time to apply my makeup. Mascara. Eyeliner. Finally, a sweet peach stain on the lips—cute, matches my skin tone. The clock keeps ticking.

The minutes pass relentlessly on full digital display on the dash clock. At the next red light, it's already 8:27. Three more minutes. I won't make it on time.

My boss is really particular about punctuality. I hope he won't be mad at me. But then: a message from him. Damn!

He wants to know where I am.

Usually, I arrive at the office around 8:00 to make myself a cup of tea before the day starts.

"A request, Miss Waverley, could you kindly pick up the breakfast I ordered from the nice little café across the street and bring it to me? I have an important meeting at 9."

I text back right away: "Happy to! Leaving now."

Oh, this is perfect...

"Very good, I'll be a bit late today. Please prepare everything."

"Gladly." My heart. Oh God, my poor heart! How much luck can one person have? Fate seems to be on my side.

I rest my forehead against the steering wheel and ignore the angry honking from the driver behind me.

Take it easy.

I need a moment to catch my breath, and then I keep driving. It's just a few more miles to the café. Once there, I pick up the order and place the food on the back seat. It's packaged in pretty, sturdy practical boxes.

Now I just need to drive to the company and act as if I've been there the whole time.

Being the boss's PA has perks. No one really questions where I am or where I've been. I've worked hard to earn this position and respect. In this industry, you can't show any weakness or uncertainty, otherwise you're an easy target. Especially as a woman.

Fourteen percent female staff. Two women in tech. The rest are secretaries or accounting. Outnumbered and underestimated, and that's just sad.

So, it's important to try to radiate presence and strength without coming across as snappy or catty. Unfortunately, people call you that quickly when you're a woman trying to assert yourself. In reality, I'm very insecure and quiet, but at work, I try to be someone I would like to be. A little more self-confidence would do me good. Fake it 'til you make it and all that.

At 8:41, I slide into my parking spot. I swap my sneakers for uncomfortable black heels I fish from the passenger footwell. Over time, you get used to being three inches taller, but I prefer walking in flats. They're so much more comfortable, but I have to suck it up as there's no way around it. The dress code requires it, and white sneakers just don't go with a business look.

I grab my handbag and go to the back seat to pick up the four boxes. I nudge the door shut with a skillful hip swing and lock the car with the remote.

Made it.

From now on, I'm setting two alarms. This won't happen to me again. I really don't want this stress again. What a lousy start to the day. But hey! I made it, and everything turned out fine in the end. Maybe this will even be the best day of my life? Who knows?

Chapter 2

Alexander

I'm on my way to the company, and according to my GPS, I should be there in about twenty minutes.

A call comes in. It's Marc, and I hit accept. My phone is connected to the car, and the hands-free system activates with a touch.

"Hey, how are you?" I ask.

My best friend was actually supposed to call me earlier, but I completely understand that he wanted to enjoy his wedding night and the following Sunday. The interruption during the ceremony had been catastrophic enough. Stephanie had nearly called everything off and walked away but fortunately, we were able to salvage the situation, and everything turned out well in the end.

"Better," he mumbles and yawns. "Stephanie's still asleep. I snuck out."

"I'll be at the office in about twenty," I announce.

"I don't plan on talking your ear off for that long." Marc chuckles. In the background, there's clattering and clicking. He's probably making himself coffee. "Man, what a night. And the one before wasn't bad either," he admits, amused. "Your tip was worth its weight in gold," he adds.

"Told you so," I reply with a broad grin.

They'd both abstained from sex for a month and even slept in separate beds. They definitely had a lot to make up for in the two nights after the ceremony.

"But she brought up that crazy woman again. I think she's still a bit unsettled. What am I supposed to do now?"

He sounds a little annoyed, but mostly just as insecure as his wife is.

"I memorized the license plate but my buddy from the police hasn't gotten back to me yet," I tell him. "He doesn't start his shift until later today. As soon as I find out who she is, I'll pay her a visit. It would be best if she apologizes to Stephanie personally and clears up the situation."

"If a guy had shown up, I'd probably have doubts too. Honestly. I really understand where she's coming from."

"Trust is good, control is better," I quote.

"Man, I would never cheat on her. She's my dream woman," he gushes and then adds: "I would fall apart if she started something with another guy."

"That's called love," I say as I stop at a red light. The traffic in London is a disaster, but not nearly as bad as in New York. But I had a driver there.

That's what I get for wanting to drive myself to be more independent and take my favorite sports car.

"Yeah," he says dreamily, which makes me smile.

"If the marriage lasts, don't forget my medal," I remind him. "A bet's a bet."

I'd been convinced the two of them would make the perfect couple, and he thought their relationship wouldn't last three years. After eight months of them dating and right before a romantic wedding, we'd changed the terms to three years of marriage. If they divorce before that, he wins. If not, I get a medal that he'll get made for me. "It has to be gold," I place my order.

"And so heavy it'll knock you to the ground," Marc says, laughing. The coffee maker in the background starts to rattle.

"I'll work out even harder so I can wear it with pride," I joke and continue driving.

"I want to thank you again, Alex," he says, then adds with a slightly melancholic tone: "For introducing me to Stephanie and setting us up, and of course for the financial jumpstart. Without you, I'd still be a single loser who gets rejected by banks. And now? Look at me. I'm living like a king."

"A king who still uses the coffee maker from his student days."

I'd recognize that rattling and clicking anywhere.

"It does what it's supposed to," he defends the old thing.

"That alone should be proof enough for Stephanie. You don't easily part with things that mean something to you."

"I'm just afraid if I compare her to my coffee maker, she'll be damn mad."

Yeah, he should probably avoid that.

"I better make sure I'm on time. My father hates it when people are late, and especially if it's me."

"You're the epitome of punctuality," he jokes sarcastically. "How many alarms did you have to turn off this morning?"

"Nine."

"Nine?" he asks, shocked.

"I just hate getting up so early. Why does he schedule the meeting at such an ungodly hour?" The sun feels like it rose just five minutes ago. "A week ago, I'd just been coming home at this hour. And I already suffer by jetlag from hell," I complain.

"Hey, we specifically scheduled our wedding for last weekend so it would work with your timing," he points out.

"And I'm really grateful for that. I wanted to enjoy New York to the fullest and thoroughly say goodbye to all the amenities." I can't help but grin broadly as I say this.

"The eternal bachelor."

"You know it."

"Stephanie has a lot of friends, I could ask her..."

"Definitely not."

"Well, I know that some of the bridesmaids found you damn hot," he reminds me.

I did notice that, but they were practically family. I've known Marc since school and Stephanie is a very good friend, so her cousins, sisters, and friends are part of the inner circle. *Never fuck the company,* as they so nicely say. I count them among the company, so no, it would be kind of weird. So, I'm not even touching that.

"London has beautiful women and tourists. And if I feel like a hot Italian, I can just hop on a plane to Rome."

"Do you feel like a second bet?" Marc sounds excited, but I sense trouble.

"Depends."

"On what?"

"On whether I have a hundred% chance of winning it. Otherwise, I'm not getting involved."

I handle my private life the same as I do my job: *Risk minimizes my interest.*

"Coward," he provokes me.

"Alright, shoot!" I am goaded. Least I can do is listen to what he has to say.

"In a year at the latest, you'll have a woman you want to marry."

I start laughing and almost miss the exit because of it.

"I'll do my best find the perfect woman for you," he adds.

"That'll be a full-time job that'll be ultimately hopeless," I promise him.

"Yeah, resist all you want, but in the end, I'll set you up with someone and you'll be happy. Just like me."

"Not in this lifetime. Maybe in the next one. In this one, I'm just me."

And that is successful and always busy. If I ever get reincarnated, then I can deal with love and starting a family. But not now. Not in my current form.

"Since when do you believe in that stuff?" he asks.

"I don't."

"You're such an idiot," he says, and I grin.

"So, how do you like London these days?"

"Eh, it's just London," I say, and my mood immediately drops considerably.

"It's not so bad. After all, it's home."

"Yeah, sure, but I really miss New York. These two cities couldn't be more different. Like a steak and a vegan cutlet," I laugh. Stephanie has been vegan for some time and Marc has to suffer a bit because of it.

"I get it," he says, and we both laugh, even though I don't feel like it.

We chat a bit more about the wedding until I reach the company and park in my assigned spot.

"So, I've arrived. I'll check in later as soon as I know anything new about the license plate."

"Alright. Talk to you later."

I hang up and remove my phone from the mount, put it in my pocket and adjust my tie and my watch. As I get out of the car, I cast a critical look around. The parking lot is clean and well-maintained, and the landscaping also gives a good impression. My father insists on such details. Punctuality. Precision. Intelligence. Good manners. A well-groomed appearance. The five pillars of his success. I'll be following in his footsteps soon, and it won't be easy. To live up to his standards, I'll have to work hard.

I walk calmly toward the entrance. It's as imposing as anything I've seen in New York. He spared no expense in shaping the first impression for potential clients. For a tech company, the extravagance feels more suited to a fashion brand, but that's my father. He loves the grand and flashy. I prefer classic and simple.

The reception hall is massive, with a soaring ceiling topped by a glass dome. From here you can see all the way up to the eighth floor, the galleries lining each level clearly visible.

My gaze drifts to the black furniture arranged near the tall windows. A few employees sit there, chatting over their morning coffee. Laptops are open on the tables, phones in hand or next to them. Young, polished women in heels hurry past me. I catch a few surprised looks but ignore them.

The reception desk stands in the center of the entrance hall. Several employees are busy there, answering phones, typing at their computers, helping colleagues with questions.

I pull out my ID card, which gives me access through security and into the restricted area. As I head toward the metal detectors, guarded by several large, broad-shouldered men, I notice a woman just ahead of me. She strides toward them confidently, and they're already smiling and greeting her warmly. The people before her only received a curt nod, nothing more.

She must be someone important, but apparently not important enough to have an assistant. She's juggling four large boxes while her small handbag keeps slipping from her shoulder.

"Good morning," the security guards greet her as she walks through the checkpoint and heads toward the elevators. I pause briefly, watching her struggle to press the elevator button with her pinky finger without dropping the boxes. It's not going well, and I'm gonna help, once I get past security.

But then she turns, and for the briefest second our eyes meet. I can't believe my eyes: It's her! The woman who almost ruined my best friend's wedding.

Chapter 3

London

I need an assistant for things like this, but I can hardly ask my boss for that. I'm carrying boxes of delicacies every day. I sigh and poke around trying to find the button. Not so easy when you only have your pinky available. I fumble around the metal wall and could swear the button is somewhere there. Damn it. I'm about to humiliate myself if I can't manage this soon. Come on! Where is this stupid button? This can't be happening!

I glance around to see if anyone's watching that I'm struggling to call the elevator, or if I can continue trying undetected. Everyone seems to be going about their business.

Only one person is looking at me. A guy in a dark brown suit. Not just watching, staring. And narrowing his eyes at me.

Oh damn! I know him: that's the guy who chased me out of the church at the wedding on Saturday. He found me? How on earth did he find out where I work? Panic surges and I immediately totter back toward the security desk. He absolutely cannot be allowed in here!

The boxes suddenly don't matter anymore. This guy is a much bigger problem.

"Raul? Hey, that guy in the brown suit. Don't let him in under any circumstances, got it?" I don't take my eyes off him, nervously watching his every move. "Throw him out!"

I need to figure out what to do in peace. If he starts yelling at me here, I might as well start looking for a new job right away.

Raul nods, and I scurry back to the elevator and manage to make it in just as two women step inside. As the doors close, I catch one last glimpse of him approaching Raul. I'm safe.

Phew, that was close. I've gotten rid of him. For now, at least.

As soon as I've delivered the order, I'll go back downstairs and speak with security. I sincerely hope they were able to get rid of him and he doesn't show up a second time.

How persistent can one man be? I already apologized. It was a mistake. Damn it, this is exactly what happens when I ignore Vanessa's advice. My fault.

Upstairs, I head straight for the small kitchen. A few employees scatter. Some employees quickly scatter as they probably don't want to be caught slacking off. I've never had friends here, just suck-ups and brown-nosers, which I hated from the start.

This is the top floor, where all the important men work. Each has multiple secretaries. Only my boss has just one: me. I've never taken a sick day. I simply couldn't afford to be. Even with a fever and chills, I showed up and served him his coffee. You just pull yourself together, grin and bear it. I couldn't have worked my way up to this high position any other way. After all, I earn incredibly good money and made myself indispensable. I could never have achieved this otherwise.

My hands shake as I arrange the sandwiches and canapés on a tray, thankful that the lettuce and veggie garnishes that came with them make them look presentable. I carry the delicious-looking snacks to the big conference room, setting everything neatly on the side table. Then I make sure the room is properly prepared. Is the trash can empty? You can't always rely on the cleaning staff. The curtains need to be tied back, and the armchairs should be positioned neither too close nor too far from the table. This room is only for Mr. Blackthorns most distinguished guests. It looks more like a luxurious gentlemen's lounge: black furniture, dark walls, gold emblems. Even the small side table probably costs more than all my furniture combined.

I smooth my hand over the backs of the armchairs, double-check the table doesn't wobble, then make a round to ensure the first impression is right: because it has to be perfect. Absolutely perfect.

But as I turn toward the door, there he is.

No, not my boss, Mr. Arthur Blackthorn, but that crazy stalker!

I gasp in panic and freeze, folding my hands together.

I immediately send a prayer heavenward while wondering how he managed to get past Raul and the rest of the security staff.

Such a damn mess. I'm done for. That's it.

His dark glare doesn't waver as he steps inside and closes the door behind him without breaking eye contact with me. I have time to study him while mentally drafting my will.

Dark brown suit with a luxurious gold watch flashing from beneath his cuff, matching his gold cufflinks. A silk handkerchief is tucked into his breast pocket.

He seems flawless. Strict. Perfect. Posture upright. Unwavering gaze.

No, this is not a stalker. This is a man you shouldn't contradict. I swallow nervously.

"How did you get in here?" I demand, trying to appear ready for a fight. I can't show any weakness!

"So you work here?" He evades my question.

"Yes. Unlike you."

He prowls the room like a predator. As if he's hunting and I'm easy prey, cutting off my only escape route.

"Then I'll fire you," he says coolly, sending chills down my spine.

"You clearly don't know who you're dealing with," I tell him sternly.

"I could say the same to you," he replies.

I narrow my eyes and study him again. Could he be a client? An important business partner I don't know about? I'm always one hundred% prepared for all guests. I know their backgrounds, their spouses' and children's names, allergies, and important phrases in their languages, customs, or little quirks.

I've never seen him before.

I would have noticed him. Definitely.

"My boss would have told me about you," I counter then and take a few steps. I notice the small delicacies on the table and remember that the order was rather spontaneous. It would be the first time in the last three years that my boss hasn't warned me about a meeting with an important client. So he must be his guest.

Damn it.

If they get along well and he's important to my boss, I could actually lose my job.

"So, you have absolutely no idea who I am? Figures. Fits the pattern that you're clueless."

He continues to stare at me sternly as he approaches me. I don't back away but keep walking across the dark wooden floor. He reaches for a canapé. Naturally, I don't stop him. He, on the other hand, hesitates and looks back at me. "Where's the coffee?"

"I was just about to get it. Milk? Sugar?"

He gives a curt nod and strolls to the panoramic windows. I slip out quietly and quicken my steps once I'm in the hallway. How unlucky can I possibly be? Today is definitely not going to be a good day.

No, it's getting worse by the minute.

Chapter 4

Alexander

Moments earlier...

I watch the *wedding crasher* vanish into the elevator. As I approach, a tall security guard steps in my way. "Sir, I regret, but—"

I don't let him finish. I quietly flash my card and sweat beads instantly on his forehead.

"I'm so sorry, Sir! I didn't recognize you! Please. Welcome."

He immediately steps aside and gives a slight bow. I decide to ignore his faux pas and walk through security to the elevators and finally relax. I press the button and study my card before putting it away. It's only issued to family members and gleams golden.

Perhaps I should have shown my face at company events once or twice so people would recognize my face, or at least my name.

The elevator doors open, and I push the button to the top floor. As the doors close, I lean against the wall, take a deep breath, and consider what to do with this woman. If she works here, I could easily have her fired, or fire her myself. But she could sue, and that would only damage our reputation.

I text Marc: "Got her."

When I arrive upstairs, secretaries cross my path, their stares obvious. They're already undressing me with their eyes. Then I see that woman again. She's leaving a room and walking down the hallway, balancing something. I follow casually and shortly after I reach the room she's in. She's carefully arranging things and doesn't notice me at first. Then she turns around and our eyes meet.

Her shock when she sees me is priceless. No, she didn't expect me here. Especially not after she told security to throw me out. She has no clue who I really am. Which makes this all the more entertaining.

As she rushes out after our exchange, I smile to myself. Oh yes... I am very excited to make her life hell for as long as she works here.

I sink into an armchair, pop a salmon canapé into my mouth, and check my phone. Marc has replied: "Who is she? What's her name?"

"All in good time," I answer mysteriously.

After all, my next steps should be carefully considered.

Chapter 5

London

I storm into the kitchen, completely agitated, and have to collect myself first. My heart pounds so hard it makes it difficult to breathe. Exhausted, I lean against the counter and take a deep breath. Then I grab my handbag, that I've left next to one of the coffee makers. I wanted to get the appetizers and sandwiches to the meeting room as quickly as possible in case my boss arrived earlier, and I would have wasted too much time to take my bag to my desk. Now I hurry with it to my place, sit down, switch on the computer, and nearly break a fingernail pressing the button.

Hands shaking, I dig through my bag until I finally pull out my phone and turn it on. I immediately text my best friend, careful not to get caught. Even though I'm technically allowed to use my phone—and have to stay reachable for my boss—I still feel like I'm doing something forbidden. Nobody can see inside my head. Nobody knows I'm texting Vanessa right now. But it feels that way, all the same.

Me: He's here!
Nessa: What? Who's there with you?
Me: HIM! HE is here! That guy!
Nessa: What's going on? Who are you talking about?
Me: The guy from the wedding. The one who chased me to my car! He showed up at my company!
Nessa: Oh shit! Did you call security?
Me: Yes, but they let him in!
Nessa: What? Why? What happened? Tell me!
Me: He must be one of my boss's clients.
Nessa: Oh no...
Me: He's about to meet with my boss. He even asked me to bring something up for his guest. They're using the good room. The luxury room—that means he's a very important guest!

Nessa: Oh, London…
Me: I'm done for!
Nessa: Stay calm. I'm sure this can be cleared up!
Me: No, he already looked so angry and even brought it up. He's looking for trouble and wants revenge. He even said he wants to get me fired! What if he really convinces my boss to fire me?
Nessa: Yes, but how? They don't have any legal grounds. It happened in private.
Me: They could force me out, or he could offer me a severance package. I don't want to leave. I love this job!
Nessa: Can you talk to him again? If you apologize and explain the situation, I'm sure he'll understand and won't be angry with you anymore.
Me: I guess I have to try.
Nessa: You can do it. Just be sweet and friendly.
Me: But he was completely awful to me!
Nessa: Please don't snap at him.
Me: I'll try.
Nessa: Let me know how it goes, okay? Tell me right away, okay?

I heart her last message and take a deep breath before putting away my handbag and making my way to the kitchen. There I fill a coffee pot and arrange milk, sugar, sweetener, little spoons, and cups on a tray. I even remember the crispy cookies my boss likes so much.

With the well-stocked tray, I head back to the room. The door is closed, so I knock timidly.

"Come in."

Maybe my boss is already there? I open the door and see that only that guy is inside. Maybe this is my lucky break.

"That took quite a while. Do you always need this much time?" he asks arrogantly, eyes scrutinizing me.

"I'll be quicker next time," I promise pleasantly. I start to pour him some coffee, but he declines, raising his hand to stop me.

"I'll do that myself."

I step back and watch him. His movements are deliberate, calm, elegant. My eyes drift to his hands—well-groomed, with slightly pronounced knuckles.

Wow, that looks good.

When I look at him, our eyes meet again.

Now he's caught me staring!

"Is there anything else I can do for you?" I ask politely.

"No. You may leave." He stirs a small spoonful of sugar and a generous splash of milk into his cup. I'll have to remember that.

"I'd like to personally apologize to you again, Mr....?" I still don't know his name.

"It wasn't me who was supposed to get married, but my best friend," he says, taking a sip of coffee before setting the cup down. "The wedding was canceled. The bride fled. His future is ruined. And it's all because of you."

Oh damn!

I gasp in shock completely at a loss on what to say.

"If you'd just let me speak to the bride, I'd clear up the misunderstanding immediately! I went to the wrong church and—"

"As I said, you may leave." He cuts me off with a dismissive wave. No interest whatsoever in hearing me out.

"My best friend was cheated on. She was in a relationship with a man and didn't know she was the other woman. When she found out he was getting married, she wanted to warn the bride. We ended up at the wrong church. It was a mistake."

Maybe that helps?

He just looks at me silently and takes another sip. No, he's deliberately ignoring me.

"So, if you'd give me the opportunity to explain everything to the bride, then—"

I break off as my boss suddenly enters the room.

"Ah, Miss Waverley," he says, beaming at me. In high spirits, Mr. Blackthorn comes over, then notices his guest. "Good to see everything worked out. I see you've already met my son."

Yeah, that's it. Game over.

While Mr. Blackthorn *Junior* fixes me with an ice-cold look, I'm just dying inside. Damn it.

"Son?" I freeze. I knew Mr. Blackthorn has a son, but isn't he supposed to live in America? Mr. Blackthorn Senior has hardly ever mentioned him. I knew nothing about his son—appearance or name.

"Yes, my son Alexander. Have I never told you about him? I seem to recall mentioning that he lives in New York." Just barely. I hadn't even known it was New York. My boss, a bit taller than me with thick white hair, a bushy mustache, and dark eyes, pauses to think.

"It must have slipped my mind," I answer, not wanting to embarrass him. "So he's your special guest today?"

"We haven't seen each other in ages. But he's been back from America for a week now and will be living here in London." He walks over to his son, who doesn't even bother to stand up. Mr. Blackthorn looks back at me and says, "It's good you're already here. You two should get acquainted."

An uncertain glance from me, is followed by a longer one at Alexander, who's also staring at me. "What do you mean?"

"Well, I'll discuss this with my son first. Then I'll call you back in, Miss Waverley."

That's my cue to leave. But I already have a sinking suspicion about what this meeting is about, and it would be the end of me. My boss might as well tie a heavy iron chain with an anchor around my neck and throw me into the sea. I can picture it vividly. He stands there smiling, waving at me and calling out: "Bon voyage." Or something like that.

When I close the door behind me, I strain to catch anything through it. Nothing. Not a single word. Great. What a mess.

I retreat to the kitchen, load up on tea, juice, and cookies, then haul my stash back to my desk. It's just outside Mr. Blackthorn's office, usually a peaceful little corner where I can work undisturbed. Well, at least I could, if my thoughts weren't completely elsewhere.

Me: I tried. He was still ice cold. No chance. But the absolute worst part: He's my boss's son!

Nessa: WHAT?

Me: Yes! He only mentioned once that he has a son who lives in America, but I didn't know anything else about him.

Nessa: Oh God...

Me: Yeah, start praying. Maybe the old man up there will actually listen for once and help me out of this mess!

Nessa: And it's all my fault. I deliberately had you drive to the wrong church. I'm so sorry, London. Please, I need to do something. Can I come over? Maybe this guy will talk to me?

Me: This Alexander is an arrogant jerk. Self-absorbed and annoyingly good-looking. The type who always gets what he wants. That's just how these rich men are. We can forget about it. Completely.

Nessa: Do you think he'll tell his father what happened?

Me: Probably. But here's what scares me more: my boss is old and starting to get a bit forgetful, and I think he might hand the company down to his son.

Nessa: Then he would become your new boss!

Me: Yes, and that's absolutely not okay! I like my boss, he's great. But I could never get along with his son.

Nessa: When will you find out?

Me: Probably soon. I'll just have to hold back and act like I think it's the best idea ever... while secretly checking job listings.

Nessa: I'm going to stay single from now on, so this doesn't happen again.

Me: Nonsense. There are good guys out there. You just have to find them.

Nessa: Or let them find you.

I send her a picture of two stick figures hugging. Then I get to work. There's too much to do and the phone won't stop ringing. This day is officially going on my top 5 list of "days I'd rather forget."

Two hours later, Mr. Arthur Blackthorn sends a message asking me to come to his lounge. I jump up immediately and lock my computer. Then I forward the phone to the central office and walk down the hallway. I tug at my blouse and skirt, fix my hair, and finally knock on the door.

"Come in." I can barely hear it. As I open the door, I swallow one last time. If I stay composed, surely I won't burst into tears. I've never handled being yelled at well.

"How may I help you, Mr. Blackthorn?" I ask. He's sitting comfortably in one of the armchairs, looking straight at me. His son Alexander, however, still has his back to me, staring out the window.

This is my end.

The short story of London Waverley.

Unfortunately, we've already reached the end. Game over.

I close my eyes and imagine the play that will someday be written and premiered about me. Will it receive good reviews? The curtains close and the audience applauds enthusiastically.

I take a deep breath, open my eyes again, and close the door behind me.

"Please have a seat," he says, pointing to the armchair next to him.

Oh, I don't like this.

My stomach turns. I've only had cookies, tea, and juice all day, and I feel like I might throw up.

With trembling knees, I reach the armchair and sit down, while Alexander still gazes out the window.

This is what I get.

I just wanted to warn a stranger and show my friend that she's not alone.

It's my fault. I've sealed my fate and ruined my professional future.

Chapter 6

Alexander

Moments earlier…

I look at my father, who cheerfully grabs one of the appetizers and enjoys it.

"How was the wedding?" he asks, taking another big sip of coffee.

"Good," I reply shortly.

"Come on, you can give me more than that," he presses.

"Marc and Stephanie are happy, and the church was decorated with lots of flowers."

That makes my father laugh.

"You're the worst storyteller I know," he says, drinking more coffee.

"It was a wedding. Just like many others." Before he can dig for more, I ask, "Why am I here?"

"Can't a father ask his son to come home so he can be closer to his family?"

"What are you planning?" I worry he wants me to take over the company, and that doesn't fit into my plans at all. My life is headed in a different direction.

"I'd like you to get more involved in the company," he begins, and I immediately stand up. I need to look off into the distance to keep my temper in check. Unfortunately, central London doesn't exactly have a calming view. From here I can see Big Ben and the crowded streets. This city holds nothing for me. New York was my goal. That's where I built a life. Now I've landed back in the *provinces*.

"In recent weeks, I've had many conversations with potential candidates. Some inside the company, many from outside. They all have their strengths, but of course I'd prefer the company to stay in the family. As my only son, it would be your inheritance."

"I was in the process of starting my own company in New York. The program is almost complete."

"Then integrate it into ours. What's the problem?"

"I employ nine people in New York. They'd all be out of a job overnight."

"Buy them out. Compensate them. If the idea is that important to you, then that's the way. Or bring them here if you think you'll work better with them."

That makes me perk up. I look back at him as he helps himself to another bite.

"I could bring them here?"

"Of course." He gestures toward the food. "Come on, help yourself."

I sit back down and try some of the delicacies he ordered for us.

"That certainly makes things more interesting," I admit. "You were against it before. What made you take a step toward me now and actually respect my wishes?" The other candidates must have been terrible.

"Get your mother a proper Christmas gift, and we'll never speak of it again."

I get it. I'm the only one he really trusts.

"I'll talk to my employees and either compensate them generously or bring them to London." I'll call my lawyer later to draft the contracts.

"By the way, who was that woman here earlier?" I ask.

"That's Miss London Waverley. She's been my PA for three years," my father explains enthusiastically. "She's never missed a day of work. I can always reach her. She's a huge support and knows the company inside and out. Her best qualities are her punctuality and her exceptionally good manners. She's always well-groomed and well-dressed. She takes great care of her appearance. She's athletic. Slim. Never a gray hair, always subtle makeup. And she's sharp, intelligent. If I had to step away for a few days, she could hide my absence from the entire staff."

He smiles and adds, "She's the daughter I never had." I wonder if he talks about me like that when I'm not in the room.

"I assume she'll become my PA once you finally take your well-deserved retirement?"

"Well, I certainly hope so."

I raise both eyebrows at that. Does this mean my father isn't insisting I take over?

"She's never done anything wrong. You won't find anyone better."

"I'd rather hire someone new," I say.

"That wouldn't be wise," he dismisses. "Or are you worried you might fall in love with her?"

I give him a confused look, which makes him laugh.

"Yes, I admit, she's an attractive woman. Plenty of department heads have asked me if they could ask her out. But so far, I've always said no."

"For what reason?"

. If she got involved with one of my subordinates, it could cause conflicts and her work would suffer. But if you want her? Go ahead. I think you two would get along well."

"She's not my type," I dismiss, uninterested.

"Will you ever settle down?"

"Says the man who's been married five times," I shoot back, annoyed.

"It's about time. You'll be twenty-nine this year, and then what? You need a steady partner. Someone who might forgive the occasional affair, give you a few children, and take your suits to the dry cleaner."

My father has always had strange morals. "Or you find a woman like your mother, to whom I've been faithful to this day. Who would have thought, huh?"

He laughs, but I only respond dryly: "I have no intention of getting married."

"So, I'll never be a grandfather?"

"Why don't you adopt your assistant and marry her off to a man of your choice? Then she can give you grandchildren."

"Not a bad idea. At least she doesn't constantly contradict me."

He never liked that, but even as a child I had my own mind and wouldn't bend. He loves it when people tell him exactly what he wants to hear. Those kinds of puppets are worth their weight in gold to him, but I can't stand people with no backbone or character.

"Let's get back to business..."

I guess I'll have to endure this for now. At least he's given in about my employees from New York. I doubt all of them will come along. Most have families, spouses, and kids.

Two hours later, he has Miss Waverley summoned to the office.

"Give her a chance," my father says just before she walks in. I'm standing by the window while she takes a seat. When I glance at her, I notice she's tense. She tries to cover it with confidence, but the little things give her away: the nervous fidgeting with her skirt, the staring and nodding too much, the excessive blinking. Even her ears are slightly red, a sign of rising blood pressure.

Is it because of me, or is she always this nervous?

For just a second, her eyes flick toward me. Hmm. Got it. It's because of me. Not surprising. I wasn't exactly kind to her. Even at the church, in her car, she apologized. But why was she in the wrong place to begin with? I'll find out soon. Unfortunately, I won't be rid of her that quickly.

"You've probably already guessed, Miss Waverley, but I'm planning to retire soon," my father begins. I pace back and forth, hands clasped behind my back, keeping my eyes on her. Fitting, really, that her name is London. Not only is the city my problem, but now so is this woman.

"Yes, sir. How can I help you?" she asks politely.

"My son will be taking over, and he needs a capable assistant. I thought of you. He, however, isn't fully convinced of your abilities yet."

She takes it well.

"I'm sure I can convince him of my skills, sir." She stays calm, though her pulse must be racing as fast as during a marathon.

"We'd like to offer you an appropriate severance package," my father suddenly says, although that wasn't what we had discussed. London takes a calm breath and smiles.

"He wouldn't find anyone better than me," she says confidently. "The training period would consume valuable months, while I have a very good relationship with existing clients and know the daily routines of all employees." She's self-assured, I'll give her that. No tears. No drama. "I will, of course, do my best to help your son in any way I can."

My father looks at me with a smile and laughs triumphantly. "Well, what do you say to that, Alexander?"

I breathe calmly and nod briefly. "It's worth a try. Four weeks' probation. If she can't convince me of her qualities during this time, I won't extend the contract."

"I already have a permanent position," she protests politely, confidently, and with a hint of joy in her eyes.

"I have the contract here. There's a clause: As soon as my father retires, there's a special termination right regarding your job."

She swallows. She must have forgotten that, repressed it, or simply overlooked it.

"You're more thorough than I expected," she admits, which tells me she knew about the clause after all.

"The severance would be generous. Nothing to worry about, London." I call her by her first name, and she lets it pass without comment. "I'd even write you a personal recommendation—despite inadequate performance."

"You have no reason to be disappointed in me yet, Mr. Blackthorn," she answers, a slight bite in her tone. It makes me smile briefly. She's got some fight in her. Maybe she's not a puppet after all.

"The onboarding starts Monday. Which means this Friday's party will be my farewell. Of course, I'll still be around as a consultant, but from now on my son will be making the calls." He's talking about the company's summer festival. Most of it has already been planned.

"That's very sudden, sir," she says, concerned. She does seem to genuinely like my father. "Not that I don't wish you a happy retirement, but..."

"I've been thinking about it for a while. The last few months have been tough. The last few weeks, almost unbearable. It's time."

She nods briefly. "Then please tell me your wishes so I can arrange the celebration accordingly."

"Surprise me. Only my wife knows me better than you, but I wouldn't want to burden her. If it were up to her, she'd drag me out of the office today." He laughs, rising from his chair. "I'll get some work done and leave you with my son for now. Show him around and get him up to speed. Things have changed quite a bit here in recent years."

"Gladly, Mr. Blackthorn." She stands, gives a slight little bow, then opens the door for him. "May I bring you a coffee later?"

"I'd like that."

She nods to him once more and then leaves, closing the door behind him. Only now does she allow herself to take a deep breath before looking at me angrily. Combative. Not bad.

"You have no intention of keeping me on, do you? Even if I handed you the Holy Grail."

"Well, if you actually brought me that, I'd make an exception."

"It's rude to call me by my first name, *Mister Blackthorn*."

"The next four—no, five—weeks are going to be very exciting," I say, amused. "Maybe you'll quit on your own and save me the severance?"

"I've been working for your father for three years, and he runs this company with passion. If you show this kind of behavior to your clients and demonstrate a leadership style similar to how you're treating me, this company will go down the drain in no time!"

Oh, she's angry.

"If you keep being this impertinent with me, the amount of your severance pay will decrease."

I'm playing with her. My father wouldn't let me pay her too little, but I want to know how far I can push her before she'll snap. How resilient is she?

"I don't care. I'll find a new job where I'm treated well. My dignity is worth more than any money you can pay me."

Now that, I like much better.

"Why were you in the wrong church?" I ask, stepping closer without breaking eye contact. London is caught off guard. I've apparently knocked her out of combat mode.

"I pressured my best friend into telling me where her cheating ex was getting married. She didn't want me to go, and kick his ass, so she gave me the wrong address. She didn't know another wedding was happening there. I just stormed out of the car, and... chaos followed." She looks uncomfortable just retelling it.

"Stephanie was really angry for a long time. After all, the wedding never even happened," I continue my little lie, which makes her look at me uncertainly. ""But you show real remorse. That's a point in your favor. You're still in the negatives, though, London."

"Don't call me by my first name," she demands again. "I deserve respect."

"All my employees call me by my first name. . It's not about respect. If I call you London, you call me Alexander."

"You're not my boss until Monday."

"You can make this complicated if you want. That's your choice." I sit back, crossing one leg over the other with a smug smile. Her red cheeks betray her: London is about to burst with anger. She's stubborn and doesn't want to give in. Maybe it will be quite fun to tease her in the coming weeks. I think I'm going to enjoy myself.

"You're not giving me an honest chance just because of that? Because I made one small mistake?" she asks me with a hurt look. I suspect she's on the verge of shedding a few tears.

"First impressions matter. I expect my employees to behave properly even in private settings and not leave a bad impression."

"Yet you're the one treating me unfairly right now."

"These are merely the consequences of your actions," I counter, leaving her standing there speechless.

What now, Princess? How are you going to get out of this situation? Are you gonna cry and tell me about your difficult childhood? Did you grow up without a father and have to assert yourself as a little sister against older brothers? Is that what made you so tough?

Are you gonna yell at me now? Tell me what a miserable bastard I am and that I should rot in hell?

Or are you gonna beg for forgiveness again and plead with me not to be so mean to you?

Hmm, there's still a fourth option: Maybe you'll strip and offer yourself to me?

"You want war? Fine, you can have it." After one threatening look, she freezes. Then she leaves the room—and no, she doesn't slam the door. She probably just remembered her promise to my father to show me around the company.

She pauses like a statue while I sit smirking, waiting for her to turn back. And turn back she does. She straightens, pushes the door open again, and steps back.

As she does, she addresses me with a punishing glare: "I'm just going to bring Mr. Blackthorn..."

"Arthur," I correct her with a cold look.

"...his coffee quickly. Then I'll come back and show you the company, sir."

She's so stubborn. Like a mule. Maybe I shouldn't call her Princess, but Little Mule? As she walks away with her nose turned up, I notice her firm ass. Really a shame she didn't choose the fourth option.

Now the real question is: what do I do with her? Only two real choices—give her a fair chance, or amuse myself over the next few weeks and toss her out in the end.

Option three would be to get her into bed. Just once.

Smiling, I fall back into the armchair and start pondering. It would be very tempting. But I'm not a monster.

I think I'll let her decide. I'll watch. And at the end of the week, I'll know whether she deserves a chance or whether I'll have my fun instead. It's up to her.

Chapter 7

London

I'm going to poison this arrogant jerk. Slip something in his coffee, push him out the window—I don't care how, but he has to go. I didn't work three years to hand everything over to his son.

With fresh coffee in hand, I walk into Mr. Blackthorn Senior's office.
"Sir? May I ask you something?"
"Is this about your probation period, Miss Waverley?"
"Honestly, yes. I'm afraid your son isn't exactly fond of me and..."
"May I be frank with you, Miss Waverley?" he interrupts, taking a sip.
"Of course, Sir." I stay standing by his desk, hoping he'll give me some reassurance.
"If he were to fire you, it would be the stupidest decision he could ever make."
"I'm honored you'd say that." But...
"But?" He reads my thoughts.
"I love my job, and I'll miss you as my boss, if I may say so. You're very hard to replace."
"I've noticed the tension between you and my son. He wanted to stay in New York, but I summoned him here. He's not happy about it and is probably just having a bad day. If you prove what you can do and support him, he'll realize he can't fire you."
"So you're gambling with me?"
"You're the ace up my sleeve." He smiles confidently and slides a letter across the desk. I reach for it, but he holds it down with his hand, making me pull back. I notice the red wax seal.
"I've prepared a document. In your favor."
"May I read it?"
"No, not yet. It may only be opened in the event of your termination."
"Is this my severance package?"

"Indeed. The amount I've listed should compensate you significantly."

"I'd prefer to work for my money."

"I'll leave this letter with our notary. If my son offers you a permanent position, it becomes void."

"That would definitely be my preference," I admit.

"You're too honest for this world." He smiles briefly, then adds: "If he gives you trouble, get him some nut chocolate. He loves it more than anything." A valuable tip.

"I'll remember that." I nod and add, "I'll show your son around the company now and walk him through everything important so he's ready to take over Monday. I'll plan the adjustments for the summer party in honor of your departure later this afternoon."

"Very good." He turns back to his screen, and I leave the office.

Now the real question: how am I supposed to pull off new plans in four days without even knowing what he wants? He's relying on me, but what if I choose wrong—too silly, too loud, or not pompous enough? Too boring? Too action-packed?

Unfortunately, there's only one person who could help me here, and that's his son. I hate that I'm dependent on this jerk.

Back at my desk, I take a moment to breathe and drink something.

Me: S.O.S.! My boss retires Friday, and his son's taking over! My contract expires, and I need a new one that comes with probation! I just spoke with Alex—he made it clear I won't survive the four weeks!

Nessa: What? Is that even legal?

Me: I signed it like that back then. Fuck. I thought Mr. Blackthorn would be here forever, and his successor would be *department heads, a shareholder, or someone from the board. Maybe even an external manager.* That would've been easy. But this? Alex hates me!

Nessa: Is there anything I can do?

Me: No... unfortunately not. I have to show this idiot around and somehow get on his good side, so he'll keep me on. I don't want a new job—even if the severance is generous. I love it here.

Nessa: Hang in there. Please let me know if anything happens, okay?

I sigh, hide my phone in my handbag, and take it with me back to the luxury lounge where Alexander is waiting. I knock, deciding to grovel. He doesn't need to know I'm just putting on a show. The main thing is I don't lose my job.

When he calls me in, I open the door. He rises and comes toward me, but I close the door and stay by it, taking the chance to be alone with him. He watches me skeptically.

"I want to be honest," I begin my lie, silently thanking Mrs. Smith for forcing me into theater class back in school. For almost two years I was on school stages—sometimes a raven, sometimes an impatient princess, once a saleswoman throwing a head of lettuce. "I haven't behaved particularly well toward you, Alexander." Addressing him informally feels so wrong.

He lifts his head slightly, observing me without expression. A man like him is surely used to submission. Maybe this will please him. Maybe I still have a chance.

"I assume this is going to be an apology?"

"Indeed." I clear my throat, trying to act like this is the hardest thing I've ever had to do. "I can be a little hot-headed sometimes. Unfortunately, that gets me into trouble now and then, but I'm working on it."

He nods once, taking a few steps without breaking eye contact.

"I know you're not going to keep me on," I add, "and I accept the severance package."

"Is that so?" His tone is skeptical.

"It would be for the best. We didn't exactly get off to a great start, and I think the trust between us has already been damaged. You need a PA you don't automatically suspect. Still, I'll give my all and support you until my very last day. This company means a lot to me—not just the business, but especially the people. I want to leave with dignity." I smile and step closer, offering my hand in reconciliation. "So, do we have a deal?"

"Which is?" he asks.

"Pleasant weeks until my departure. I'll do my best, and you'll treat me with respect."

Alexander hesitates, then finally takes my hand. A tingling sensation rushes through me, making me shiver. His grip is warm, firm, and the scent of his cologne throwing me off balance. Why does my body react so strongly to this man? He looks at me, and I have the sudden urge to glance at his lips. Just briefly. Just for a tiny moment. Then I look back into his eyes.

"Deal," he says with a smile, and we let go.

"Okay. So, this is the luxury lounge. The most beautiful room in the entire company. We host very special guests here—wealthy clients, close friends of the family. The room is heavily soundproof. If you want someone outside to hear you, you have to raise your voice," I explain in an almost friendly manner as I walk to the cabinets. "There's also a hidden bar. Your father takes pride in his collection of fine spirits, and guests love to sample them. We stock wine, vodka, and other drinks—always with at least two spare bottles in the cellar. If anything runs out, it's reordered immediately. Only your father, security, and I have keys to the storage room. And every time the lock is opened, it's recorded. I'll show you that later."

"Why all the security?" he asks.

"Because this bottle of wine alone costs sixty thousand pounds."

"I see." He steps closer, takes the bottle from me, examines it, and sets it back. "I need an office." He scans the room. "This will do."

Will do?!

"But this is—"

"It was. You'll redesign it as my office."

"Of course. Gladly."

Born with a silver spoon in his mouth, clearly. I take a deep inconspicuous breath and show him the rest of the room's features: the air conditioning, the snack bar, the dimmable lights.

"Would you like me to introduce you to all the employees or just the department heads? I can arrange meetings in each office."

"Just the department heads and the key people who should know me."

I nod and begin our tour.

The most important offices are on the top floor—his father's, of course, along with the department heads. They rarely work from them, but they're there. The floor also has multiple conference rooms equipped for video conferences.

On floors one through seven, the various departments are located: customer service, sales, development, and more. Alexander shakes a lot of hands while department heads explain things. Every now and then I quietly feed him names and titles as we go.

"This is his deputy, Miss Carlson," I explain, for example, when she is visiting her colleagues to show off her newborn. "She had a daughter, Marie, four weeks ago. She'll be on leave until next year."

"Miss Carlson, a pleasure to meet you," Alexander greets her, glancing at the baby. "What a sweet girl." In her little green outfit, the baby could easily have been mistaken for a boy. I've just saved him from a potential faux pas.

On the ground floor, we stop at the training rooms, the reception, the kitchen, and a large cafeteria. I point out the fitness studio. "Employees can use it for free." Then the massage practice. We can treat four people at once. "This boosts morale and also helps prevent back problems. Very important to your father."

We even have a first aid station for minor injuries. "We get accidents treated here, Mostly burns from hot coffee or nausea. Pregnant women also come here when they feel unwell." The daycare is also there. "Two facilities—one for babies and toddlers up to three, another for kids up to ten. They stay here after school—we got teachers and childcare workers on staff who can help with homework or just play."

"Pets, too?" he wonders.

"Yes. A lot of employees bring their dogs so they're not home alone all day. Staff plays with them, feeds them food specified by their owners, and walks them."

"My father never mentioned any of this." Alexander lingers at the glass, watching the dogs.

"Many colleagues spend their lunch breaks visiting their pets," I explain, then gesture toward the stairwell. "Now we just have the basement and parking garage left."

He follows to the stairwell silently, while I go on, "From the start, your father wanted employees to be able to focus fully on their jobs. If a child is sick, one parent usually stays home or gets sick too. Parents don't get the chance to rest then come to work sick. He wanted to prevent that. So contracts here include more sick days than the law requires—with full pay, of course."

"And people don't abuse it?" he asks.

"There are definitely some who take advantage," I admit, "but your father doesn't want to punish those who genuinely need it. There's a lot of trust here, and it pays off. Sick days are far below expectations." I open the stairwell door and let him go through first.

"He mentioned you've never missed a day."

"I haven't been sick in three years."

"Never?" He smiles.

"Never. Just the occasional cough, a little sniffle, sometimes a headache. Manageable."

"You're very loyal to my father. How much does he pay you?"

"Eight thousand pounds a month," I answer. "Very generous."

"Any other benefits?" We descend the stairs, signs pointing to the underground garage.

"Fourteen monthly salaries, plus allowances for trips abroad."

In the basement, I show him the storage rooms where we stash both old computers and new equipment, the technical room, heating and cooling systems, and other storages with items important for the company: from towels to medical products, office chairs to planters in case new plants are bought or someone knocks one over and it breaks.

"Okay, I've seen enough. Organize meetings with each department head. Individual sessions starting tomorrow at 10, ending at 4. Thirty minutes each, no breaks except lunch—1:30 to 2:30."

"There are eighteen department heads," I point out.

"I'll be here all week."

"Friday we finish at one. At six, everyone is going to meet at a Country Inn in Mickleham for the summer party. We hold it there every year."

"A country inn?" He walks to the elevator that comes all the way to the basement and presses the button.

"Yes. All four hundred and six colleagues from the London HQ are invited, though only three hundred and forty-four accepted. The rest are on sick leave, vacation, or parental leave."

Alexander looks amazed.

"There's a buffet in the hall, with tables, and the kitchen. In the garden outside, there are festival tents, barbecue spots, and several lounge areas fully equipped with garden furniture and recliners," I explain. "It rained last year here and there, which is when we use the hall, but if the weather's good, most of it is outside. There's a live band and a screen that will be used in the evening before your father gives his farewell speech."

The elevator doors open. To my surprise, he politely lets me go first. I press the top button, the doors close, and it begins to rise.

"Today I'll retreat to a side office and familiarize myself. I'll make calls, and don't want to be disturbed. Tomorrow I start with the department heads." He takes out his phone. "Your number?"

I pause, caught off guard because I wasn't expecting it. But I give him my number, and he saves it.

"Would you like to move into the lounge now or another office first?"

"Temporary office today. Tomorrow I'll move into the lounge. I'll be here at eight. I take my coffee—"

"With a teaspoon of sugar and a splash of milk," I cut him off.

His brows rise in surprise, then he nods.

Upstairs, I settle him in an empty office and bring him a company laptop and a cup of coffee.

"Is there anything else I can do for you?" I ask nervously, standing at the door while he's already working on the laptop.

"Not for now. I'll let you know."

"Okay. I'll be at my desk."

I leave and arrange for someone from the tech team to have the lounge refitted. A large wooden desk, full with a computer system is brought in, along with a leather chair, and several items to properly setup the office. In the meantime, I tackle scheduling the eighteen meetings with the department heads. They're all very busy and their schedules sometimes overlap, so I need to juggle about, but this is my bread and butter. It takes nearly two hours to set up a schedule that fits everyone's calendars, but finally the invitation emails are sent. One task down.

After lunch I'll continue planning. It's taking up most of my day at the moment, but I'm also really looking forward to it.

Now I stretch, log off, and send Mr. Arthur Blackthorn a quick message that I'm going on break. I copy it and paste it into Alexander's chat. My first message to him—crazy that he has my number now.

Just as I'm about to go, he texts back.

Curiously, I look at my phone while slinging my bag over my shoulder.

"Can you recommend a restaurant?"

"There's a café across the street. I picked up the canapés and sandwiches from there this morning. Big selection," I text back and heat out.

Most employees eat in the cafeteria or at food stalls around the building, but I prefer the juice bar across the street. They have fresh salads, smoothies, wraps, and fruit bowls.

His next text comes in as I reach the elevator. *"Are you going there?"*

"No, somewhere else."

"Address?"

Damn it. I just want my peace and quiet during my break.

"To The Fruit Bar, one street over," I type.

He doesn't respond further. Hopefully he won't get any ideas to follow me. I like this sweet little juice bar. It's unassuming and cozy. The perfect place to relax.

By the time I reach the ground floor, reception improves, and another text comes through: *"Sounds good."*

Yes, it does. That's why I eat there—alone. But I don't want to say that.

I quicken my pace toward the exit, but Raul from security steps in my way.

"Ah, Miss Waverley. About Mr. Alexander Blackthorn."

"Yes?" I adjust my handbag.

"I had to let him through. You understand, right?"

"Of course. I didn't recognize him at first. Everything's fine," I promise him.

"Oh, good. So, I won't get in trouble?" This big guy, shoulders as wide as a bus, mid-twenties and looking dangerous, but with a heart of gold, is actually worried?

"No, of course not. You were just following my instructions. Everything's fine, Raul," I assure him.

"Oh, That's a relief."

He steps back and gives me a polite nod. I smile, then walk through the security gate, finally heading out for my well-deserved break.

As soon as I leave the building, a message from Vanessa pops up: *Are you on break? Wanna chat on the phone?*

"Yes, soon," I text back. *"Will call you. Eating."*

Typing while walking isn't that easy.

I roll my eyes while I wait at the crosswalk because of course Alexander is texting me too: "*Can you send me photos of their selection?*"

So, he wants me to pick something up. Technically, this is my break—the only sixty minutes I get to myself during the workday without my boss breathing down my neck. But fine. I'll be nice.

"*Sure,*" I reply, hurrying across the street. Even walking fast, I reach the other side just as the light flips red again. Who sets these timers, seriously? I sigh and head toward the juice bar. It's less than a minute away, even in heels on the uneven sidewalk.

At the Fruit Bar, only a few people are in line. A shame, really. People line up for greasy pizza, fries, and burgers, but a place serving fresh, healthy food barely gets noticed. While that means there's more for me, I can't help worrying they won't stay in business for much longer.

I snap a few photos of the sandwiches, bagels, salads, wraps, smoothies, and the delicious bowls, then send them to Alexander. Then I step in the line. The staff, of course, know me by now and we nod to each other politely. I keep checking my phone, but Alexander doesn't respond.

"I'm up next," I text him, but he sends nothing. Should I just order something random, or has he lost his appetite?

"That looks really good." His voice suddenly comes from right behind me. I inhale sharply, spinning around. How did he get here so fast?

"Let me treat you," he says.

"Really?" I ask, stepping closer to the display case.

"Yes." He watches me as I turn to the saleswoman.

"Hi, uhm, I'll take the chicken wrap, the large watermelon bowl, and a salad."

"Large or small?" she asks.

"Large. Oh—and a mango smoothie too, please." If he's paying, I might as well go all out.

"I'll have the same," Alexander says, pulling out two crisp fifty-pound notes from his black wallet. "Keep the change as your tip." He throws in a charming smile and a wink, which pretty surely sets the young server's heart racing. She's completely taken with him.

"Would you like to eat here?" she asks him, no longer paying any attention to me.

"To go, please," I say firmly. That gets her attention back on me.

"Where do you eat?" Alexander asks.

"At a super-secret location," I answer cryptically.

"Which you're definitely going to tell me about, right?" He asks as he tucks his wallet away.

"I like to spend my break alone," I tell him.

"I thought you wanted to apologize to Marc. He'll be available on the phone soon." Alexander raises his eyebrows provocatively.

I hesitate. Damn. That would indeed be a good opportunity.

"Just this once," I say, then look at the server who—if I didn't know better—has heart eyes. Maybe *she* can work for him. Coincidentally, a position will be opening up in four weeks.

I stand silently beside Alexander while our order is packed. When I reach for it, he takes most of the bags like a true gentleman.

"So, you eat healthy?" he asks.

"Usually." I really don't want to talk to him. "I eat on the company roof," I explain. "Only a few people have keys. When I started working here, there was this project called *Green Roof*."

"I remember. My father told me about it," he says, then casually shifts to the outer edge of the sidewalk, closer to the street. At first, I wonder what he's doing, until I remember an article I read—apparently, men who care always walk street-side to shield women from danger.

Okay. That earns him a very small point in his favor. A tiny one.

Chapter 8

Alexander

She looks frazzled. I can see exactly how uncomfortable my presence makes her. Of course, I'm milking it a little—she deserves it.

As we head back to the main building, I text Marc: "*Got the wedding crasher with me. She's my father's PA. I'm supposed to take over the company soon, so she'll be working for me. I'll probably fire her after the probation period. I told her the wedding didn't happen. She feels guilty.*"

Marc replies: "*Seriously?*"

I text back" *Yeah. We're on lunch break. She's about to call you to apologize. Forgiving her is up to you.*"

I slip my phone away as we step inside.

Security wave us through, and we head toward the elevator.

"You need a code to get to the roof," she explains. "Eight digits."

"My mother's birthday," I say, watching her. She clearly already knows. It only earns me a small smile.

The doors close, and the elevator starts moving. The doors open onto a dark little room. London swipes a card, punches in the code, and with a loud CLACK, the lock releases, and she pushes the door open.

Sunlight floods into the dark hallway, a small box-like structure, and we step onto the rooftop. A five-foot wall surrounds a wild green oasis—moss, grass, and pure wild growth everywhere. Bees buzz alongside other insects. Birds seem to love it too.

In the middle of London's little paradise stands a wooden bench, the only thing not overgrown with plants. Stone slabs form a narrow path toward it.

"Why isn't this open to everyone?" I ask.

"Because they'd trample everything. Your father gave me the code so I could have my breaks in peace. He figured out how much I need nature. Not much of that here in the city."

"How'd he figure that out?"

"During my interview. After the tour, he asked what I'd change. He promised that if I survived the three-month probation, he'd green the roof just for me. He kept his word even before the time was up."

Her smile is grateful as she sits. I drop down beside her, pulling out my phone, and just like that, her mood sours.

"Do you want to eat first or call Marc right away?" I set the two bags down between us—smoothies, wraps, salads. She carried the deep, wide bowls.

"I'd rather get it over with," she admits, looking incredibly nervous.

I dial Marc and hand her my phone. As she takes it, I put it on speaker.

"Hey, Alex?" Marc's voice comes through.

"Uh, no. This is London Waverley. Alexander's father's assistant. The... wedding crasher. Alex was kind enough to let me use his phone to call you and apologize. I'd also like to explain and maybe talk to Stephanie to save your marriage."

Marc stays quiet, letting her squirm. London fidgets with her skirt, her ears and cheeks turning scarlet.

"Hmmm... Well, if you want to talk to Stephanie, sure. She still doesn't fully believe I don't know your friend."

"I'm so, so sorry. I thought I was crashing *that idiot*'s wedding..." London starts pouring her heart out. She explains in detail about how her best friend Vanessa found out she was the other woman, and how they just wanted to warn the bride. "But she had the wrong church," she chatters on, without Marc having even the slightest chance to respond.

"Okay. I believe you," he says, giving in surprisingly quickly. "Convince my wife, and I'll forgive you."

"Wife?" she asks, puzzled.

"We still got married." Marc chuckles.

London's glares at me soon after.

"Oh, really? Did you?"

I grin broadly. "Seems you misunderstood something." I can't help laughing. She absolutely fell for it. She presses a hand to her chest, breathing in deeply.

"Thank goodness. And yes, I would really like to speak with Stephanie. Is she there?"

"She's at the salon. But I'll let her know and text Alex later," Marc says.

"Okay. Thank you so much..." London sighs with relief and then says goodbye: "Um, see you later then. I'll give you back to Alex." She hands me the phone.

"Bye," I say flatly and hang up. Her brows shoot up at my bluntness, but I'm already taking the food out of the two bags and place it between us.

"You tricked me," she growls, immediately snatching a wrap away from me.

"Yes," I admit, smiling and amused.

"That wasn't nice."

"Neither was storming a church and causing chaos."

"Are you going to hold that over me forever?"

"For a while longer. At least until you stop getting so worked up about it." I bite into the wrap, which is absolutely delicious. I think I'll have lunch there more often. The cute server wasn't bad either and could keep me company for an evening.

"Are you always this hot-tempered?" I ask.

"It's hard to stay calm in certain situations, especially when it involves my friends or people I care about," she admits. However: "I'm not like that at work."

"Just a few hours ago you were threatening me with war." I remind her, amused. Her ears and cheeks flame again.

"You provoked me."

"You let yourself be provoked."

"It's a tough situation. You're my boss's son, and…" She drops her gaze, staring at her barely-touched wrap. "If I hadn't stormed into that church, if I'd just listened to my friend, then…" She trails off, breath hitching.

"Then what?"

"We would have met under normal circumstances. You would've gotten a good impression of me, and I'd still have my job—a job I honestly love more than anything. One mistake, and my career's ruined."

Oh, is she angling for sympathy? I can't tell how serious she is.

"If Stephanie forgives you, then I will too. It was her wedding. I was just the best man."

As I say this, her gaze immediately shifts to me. Her large dark brown eyes shimmer as if tears are forming.

"Really?" she breathes in disbelief. I think she's just putting on an act. Women like to do that to stir up sympathy, to trigger a man's protective instinct. That's what she'd be doing—if I were falling for it. Still, I do feel a little sorry for her. If Marc and Stephanie aren't angry anymore, then I'll forgive her too. Maybe she could be useful as my assistant after all?

"Yes," I assure her, which leads her to breathe a sigh of relief before smiling and then enjoying her wrap. Hmm. I don't know. Maybe she's sincere after all.

Chapter 9

London

I think he's falling for it. Though, honestly, not everything I said was an act. Maybe a genuine fresh start wouldn't be such a bad idea. Of course, I'll apologize to Stephanie properly and hope she's not angry still.

I sneak glances at Alexander every now and then. The fact that he knows about my favorite spot makes me uneasy. I suspect he'll show up here often now, which means I won't have my breaks to myself anymore.

We enjoy our meal until it's time to head back to the office. We leave the roof and take the elevator one floor down to the eighth floor.

"By the way, you can move into your office now," I tell him as we step out. "If you need anything, just press one on your phone and you'll be connected to me. If I don't answer, after six rings it'll go to the main switchboard. You can also call my cell anytime."

"Anytime?" he asks with a smug smile.

"Half an hour before work starts and half an hour after it ends. Outside those times, only if it's an absolute emergency." I try to remain calm and polite, even though I suspect he's hinting at something more specific. He's probably testing if I'm available for... that kind of thing. Not happening. Especially not with him.

"I'll keep that in mind," he says, which is a relief.

We reach his new office. Not much has changed, but he seems pleased. Alexander scans the room, checks the desk, then nods.

"Very good. I'll settle in and reach out if I need something."

I nod politely and start to leave, but he stops me. "Could you bring me a coffee?"

"Of course." The trials of being a young assistant. I'm basically a walking coffee maker.

I stop by my boss's office first. If he wants one too, I can kill two birds with one stone. I then head to the kitchen. While the machine brews,

I get lost in thought as I prepare the cups and wait for the machine to finish brewing.

What can I do to keep this job?

If I apologize sincerely to this Stephanie, and if Alex gives me a fair chance, maybe this will work. I'll just grit my teeth and show my best side. It won't be easy. I just need to make sure I keep my emotions in check and don't act impulsively. Sometimes my mouth is unfortunately faster than my brain. I sigh quietly, pour the coffee into cups, and head back.

I serve my boss first, then bring Alexander his. He's at his desk, working. That's when I notice a USB drive beside his laptop.

"Here you go," I say, setting the cup down. "Wouldn't an external hard drive be better? Those little things don't hold much."

"It's my lucky charm. I've carried it forever." Alexander picks it up and turns it in his hand almost reverently before setting it back down next to the laptop.

Got it. Everyone has their quirks.

He looks at the coffee. "Thank you, London." He smiles, takes the cup, then asks, "Do you actually like your first name?"

"Yes, I do." I don't want to get into this with him.

"I spoke with Stephanie. She'd like to meet you. How about tomorrow evening? They leave for their honeymoon Wednesday, so it's perfect timing."

"Yes, that works. Right after work?"

Oh man, I'd rather avoid this meeting altogether. But I have to get through it now. Maybe she's actually nice, and I'll get off with just a black eye.

"Can I give her your number? Then you two can set it up directly."

"Yes, of course." I try to mask how nervous I feel. "Do you need anything else?"

"No, thank you for the coffee." He lifts the cup and takes a sip.

I say goodbye and head back to my desk. There's still so much to do.

A whole lot.

In the afternoon, I'm so focused on my work that I lose track of time. It's only when colleagues start heading out and the office takes on that end-of-day hush that I notice I'm already four minutes past clocking off. I stand, stretch, and head toward my boss's office. Looks like he's working late today. But when I knock, there's no answer. So I turn toward Alex's office instead.

The door is slightly ajar, and that's when I hear voices—my boss and Alexander talking inside.

"Are you absolutely sure?" my boss asks his son. If Mr. Blackthorn didn't sound so alarmed, I probably would have knocked. But instead, I stand there, trying to breathe as quietly as possible.

"Yes, of course. She already admitted it, apologized, and everything's fine for now," Alexander says, reassuring him. My stomach twists. They're definitely talking about me. Which means now my boss knows. Damn.

"This is outrageous!" my boss snaps. I've never seen him this angry. My heart sinks to my knees, and I start trembling.

"You will fire her!" my boss demands. And with that, my heart plummets to the floor.

"I can't do that," Alexander defends me.

"Why not? You can never trust someone like that again!" I'm finished. Done for. That's it. I thought things with Alexander could work out, but if even my own, usually gentle boss is against me, I might as well kiss my job goodbye.

"But she needed it, and she promised to return it to me."

Wait, what?

I lean closer, as Alexander explains further. That doesn't sound like me at all. What exactly did I need? And what am I supposed to return?

"As if she would have done that. And in her first probationary week, no less," my boss hisses. "No, trust me, son. You need to fire her. There are plenty of good housekeepers out there. Someone like this needs to be dismissed immediately!"

Housekeeper?

"She does excellent work otherwise. I trust her."

"And she's abused that trust. How much are you even paying her monthly?"

"She gets two thousand pounds. She only comes to my place twice a week, about four hours each time."

Wow, that's what I call good pay.

"So, eight hours a week?"

I quickly do the math. Whoa! She earns more than I do. That's an impressive sixty-two and a half pounds per hour.

"Yes," Alexander confirms.

"I don't even pay London that much, honestly. What on earth made you decide to give her such a high wage?"

Yes, I'd like to know that too, and where I can apply. That would be a great supplementary income.

"She has a young son and a sick sister," Alexander replies.

"Yes, they always do. And then she steals cash from you?"

"She desperately needed it and didn't dare ask me for an advance," Alexander says, sounding annoyed.

"It's your house, your decision," my boss sighs. "But I'm telling you: This woman will cause trouble. Big trouble."

I hear footsteps moving toward the door, so I back away quickly and step into the hall, pretending I just arrived as my boss opens it.

"Oh! Mr. Blackthorn, there you are. I've been looking for you. Is there anything else I can do before I go?" I act sweet and innocent while scraping my heart off the floor and stuffing it back into my chest.

"Ah, Miss Waverley. I'm glad to see you." He seems relieved and pats my shoulder. "I can always count on you." He shakes his head. "No, I've got everything, thank you. Finish up for the day. Today was a long one."

"Very well, Mr. Blackthorn. I'll check if your son needs anything, and then I'll head home."

"Excellent. See you tomorrow."

He walks down the hallway back to his office, allowing me to catch my breath before going to Alexander. I close the door behind me, though.

"I was just about to wrap up. Do you need anything before I go?"

Alexander is leaning against his desk, long legs stretched out. He sets aside a glass of mineral water. He could've called me for that, couldn't he? Or maybe sometimes he likes going to the kitchen himself. I'll have to figure that out.

"You were eavesdropping." He says it matter-of-factly, not angry, not even surprised. I draw a breath, ready to deny it, but then he smirks. "Your shadow was visible on the door."

Well, no point lying.

"So... your housekeeper stole from you?" I ask carefully.

"So you *were* eavesdropping." He laughs. "I thought maybe I'd imagined it."

Damn. Next time I should at least feign innocence.

He looks amused. "How much did you hear?"

"That she earns more than I do and still helped herself anyway," I admit through clenched teeth.

Alexander smiles. "Her story touched me. I wanted her to earn well and still have time to care for her son and her sick sister."

"How much did she steal?" I press.

"Twenty thousand pounds."

My eyes go wide.

"I kept it in a box. She found it while cleaning and took it. I had planned to use that cash, and when I checked, it was gone. I confronted her, and she confessed immediately."

"Well, denying it would've been pointless. Unless other people come and go in your house..." I let the question hang, fishing for more. A relationship, maybe?

"She was the only one. But she promised to pay me back—either through a loan or monthly installments." He doesn't sound convinced.

"Do you believe her?"

He looks at me and says: "If I'm being honest: I think she's long gone."

"Do you have her number?"

"Yes, but she hasn't answered since yesterday. Still, I want to trust she'll be back by this weekend." He pulls out his phone and types on it briefly before reading aloud. Then he reads a message aloud: '*You can pay it off in small installments, every month. And if one month doesn't work out, then the next. We'll figure it out—don't worry.*'

"Hmm..."

I wouldn't have pegged him as so lenient. That makes me uncertain. Could this guy actually be one of the good ones?

"My father calls me naive, and if I told Marc or my other friends, they'd call me crazy. Maybe I am. But I wanted to give her a chance. My father was always very strict with the staff. My mother too. Once..." He studies me, then adds: "You're off the clock."

"I'm also a good listener." I walk toward him slowly and notice he doesn't have much water left in his glass. I open the mini fridge, grab the bottle, and refill it.

"Thank you. So..." He ponders briefly, then continues: "We had a maid who was fired on the spot when my mother found out she had stolen from the cash box."

"How much?" I ask as I put the bottle away.

"Just a few hundred pounds. I liked her. Elaine to me was like a big sister. I must've been ten or eleven, she was in her early twenties. She needed the job. Her mother was sick, her father had died, and she was the family's only breadwinner. Debts piled up. She even skimped on food. When my mother threw her out, I tracked her down and gave her all the money I'd saved."

"So that's why you trust your housekeeper?"

"Yes. Because not every person is evil. Everyone has their story. Who knows what happened that she couldn't resist when she found the money? Maybe she also has debts or something urgent to fix." He looks thoughtful.

"How did you find her to hire?"

"In the newspaper. Very traditional. She made a good impression, so I hired her right away. My house is big—I figured a woman's touch couldn't hurt. She was just supposed to dust and clean the floors and windows. Not much. I can take care of the rest myself."

"I hope she shows up at your place on Saturday," I say, giving him a small smile.

"Has Stephanie contacted you yet?" he asks, changing the subject.

"Honestly, I haven't checked. My phone's been in my bag all day. If she has, I'll call her as soon as I get home."

Alexander raises his glass to me. "Stephanie's my best friend. I've known her forever. She has a good heart. If you don't threaten to make her life a living hell, you definitely have a chance." He's probably going to hold that against me forever.

"Thanks for the tip," I mumble, embarrassed, then leave his office. As I go, I see him finish his glass and circle around his desk.

Phew. What a day. What an incredible situation. I honestly thought he'd fire his housekeeper on the spot or call the police. But this man actually has a good core. I wonder what else I'll discover about him.

Back at my desk, I close all my applications, shut down the computer, and take my empty teacup to the kitchen. Only then do I check my phone. Vanessa has sent me dozens of messages, but I'll deal with those later because a new number has popped up.

Nervously, I tap the chat.

Stephanie: : Hey, it's me. The bride who almost didn't get married. Alexander gave me your number. If you have time tomorrow after work, I'd really appreciate it if we could meet. Preferably at your place. I'd rather not discuss certain things in public, and Marc is here all the time.

Me: Hey. I'm really glad you want to talk to me. I want to apologize in advance and explain to you tomorrow, calmly, how this terrible mix-up happened. I'll happily send you my address. I probably won't be home until around 5:30 PM today, and maybe tomorrow too. So if you'd like to come around 6, I'll definitely have time for you. Is there anything special you'd like to drink or eat? Tea? Coffee? Cookies? Let me know so I can pick up a few things.

I grab my bag and type the last words while walking, then send the message and head to the elevator. Okay, let's see—what else do I need to do today? Shopping would be good. And go to the gym later. I really need to work out hard and get my butt in gear.

Downstairs, I say goodbye to security and head to my car. Of course, I notice the looks from others. I was never popular, but once you start paying attention, the staring is uncomfortable. I don't even want to know how bad my reputation is. Being a woman in such a high position isn't easy, and my female colleagues especially seem to need someone to hate. They probably bet on whether I'm sleeping with my boss—and now surely assume I'm going after Alexander too.

Ridiculous. They should get to know Mr. Blackthorn better. He's such a wonderful person. Well, except when it comes to theft. Or tardiness.

Okay, fine—he does have his quirks, but he's an old-school gentleman. If you behave properly, he has no reason to get upset.

I slip into my car, kick off my high heels, and massage my feet before pulling on my comfy sneakers. I'll change clothes as soon as I get home then head straight to the gym. I want to hit the treadmill, do some time on the ergometer, and strength training. The more muscles, the more I burn—which means I can eat more. And I love food.

If Stephanie replies soon, I'll shop beforehand, so I don't have to do it tomorrow after work.

Well, let's go. Home it is.

Chapter 10

Alexander

"Alexander?" she asks nervously.

At first glance, she looks like a doll come to life, but her expression gives her away—she's shy.

"Do we know each other?" I ask. Wouldn't be the first time someone came running up after a one-night stand. But I haven't been in London for what feels like an eternity, and I'd remember someone like her. Unless she completely reinvented herself. She's not really my type anyway—I go for classic elegance, not so colorful.

"My name is Vanessa. I'm London's best friend. Your PA."

Perfect. Just what I needed.

"And I take it she has no idea you're here talking to me?"

"I've been texting her all afternoon, but she hasn't replied. London gets so wrapped up in work she forgets everything else." She takes a step closer. I'm only a few feet from my car. "I wanted to apologize in person. London had nothing to do with the church incident."

"Well..." I appreciate her loyalty, but still: "As far as I remember, she stormed into the church."

"Yes, but that's my fault. I gave her the wrong address on purpose—I didn't realize a wedding was happening there. She was so determined, and I panicked. It's all on me. Please don't fire her! She loves her job!"

I sigh. "And to tell me this, you came all the way here to talk to me?"

"I took a taxi."

"You don't drive?"

"I had a few drinks." And she's been crying too. "Things are a bit rough right now," she sobs. "And now I've ruined London's career because I—" Her words dissolve into loud, bitter sobs.

"Okay, okay. Breathe." I should have some tissues in the car. I dig into the glove box, find a pack, and hand them to her. She follows me and immediately goes through two of them.

"I'll drive you home and you'll get some rest, okay?" That sounds like a reasonable idea.

She nods tearfully and I step aside so she can slip into the passenger seat. Looks like I'm taking a detour tonight, but this way I'll get to know her a bit better. With some luck, she might share some insider stories about London and give me teasing fodder.

I slide in, buckle up, then remind her: "Seatbelt, please."

"Oh—right! Yes, yes..." She needs another tissue, then she puts on her belt too. "By the way, this is a really nice car."

"Mhm," I reply, , before I start questioning her. "So, you're best friends?"

"Oh yes, since forever. We met in school and clicked right away. I was very shy back then, and London used to beat up the boys who teased me."

"Did she really?" I chuckle as I start the engine.

"Yes. She's always been a fighter. Probably because of her three older brothers."

"She has three of them?" I was spot on with my theory.

"Yeah, and they're tough as nails. Her father too. She had to learn early on how to stand up for herself, otherwise she'd have been trampled. You'd think being the youngest—and the only girl—she'd be spoiled. But nope, London was raised her like one of the boys for the first few years. Had to go on fishing trips, played soccer, and the boys would beat her up sometimes when they fought over candy." That sounds awful. "She then took up karate, later Krav Maga. Once she broke a guy's nose when he hit on us in a bar."

"Just like that?" I ask in astonishment as I pull out of the parking space. Good thing she didn't punch me. That would have been interesting.

"He grabbed my breast and her butt. Next thing, he was on the floor bleeding."

"So, she packs quite a punch?"

"Yes. But she also broke a nail. She'd just had them done, too, the day before. That was honestly the worst part of the whole thing."

"Hmm." Got it. "How long ago was that?"

"Oh, ages ago—maybe when we were nineteen or twenty," Vanessa adds with a sigh. "She's really a good person."

"Yes, I get that now. I'm not mad at her anymore. She'll apologize to the bride and groom, then it's over."

"So, you're not firing her?" she asks, looking surprised and happy at the same time.

"She's good at her job, and my father's her biggest fan. If she keeps it up, I'll probably keep her."

I don't like crying women. Or tears on leather seats. But apparently my answer sets her off again. This time, she's crying with joy.

"That sounds wonderful! Really! Oh, thank God! I haven't been able to sleep the last few nights!"

"Where do you live, anyway?" I ask, starting to drive without thinking.

"Um… we need to turn right soon, then pass Big Ben, and then… quite a bit further."

"What's the address?" When she tells me, it's no wonder she took a taxi. Public transport would have taken her at least two hours. With the car, we only need about forty minutes.

I'm lucky. Vanessa falls asleep almost immediately. At least she's not crying anymore, and I have some peace and quiet during the drive.

Forty-three minutes later, I pull up in front of her apartment building and park. She has a nice place here. Upper-middle class.

"Vanessa? We're here." I gently touch her shoulder. She grunts softly and stirs awake, rubbing her blonde mane out of her face.

"What happened?" she asks drowsily.

"We're at your place," I explain.

"Oh. Good. That was quick." She yawns, digs out her keys from her handbag, and mumbles, "You're such a nice, decent guy. I don't understand why London thinks you're so… shitty." She pats my cheek. "Thanks for the ride. See you around."

She tries the door but fails. Clearly too little sleep, and way too much to drink.

"You can tell her I drove you home. That should earn me a few points on my karma account." I unbuckle and get out. Better help her upstairs before she collapses in the stairwell.

I could totally see that happening.

I walk around the car, and open her door, but getting out doesn't quite work since she's still buckled in. I quickly fix that and carefully help her out of the car, stand her upright, and close the door. I lock the car and carefully support her, but after a few steps, she can walk on her own and doesn't need my help anymore.

"I should've met you instead of that miserable cheater," she complains desperately, tears streaming again. "How could he do this to me? Why do you men do such things?" she asks me, sobbing.

"Unfortunately, some people don't value faithfulness," I say, guiding her to the hallway. "Which floor?"

"The first."

We climb up the steps. And she fumbles with the key on her door, so I help her again. The door opens and she stumbles inside.

"I mean, just look at you. Such a good guy. Bringing me all the way home and not even trying to grope me." She says like she's proud of me and sighs softly as I guide her to her living room.

"That should be the standard. The absolute minimum," I tell her.

"A walking green flag!"

"Excuse me?" I ask.

"You're a good guy. Such a good..." She stumbles toward the couch and falls. I wasn't quick enough to catch her. But she appears to be lying comfortably and has fallen asleep again.

It was all too much for her, I suppose. I assume that adrenaline was responsible for her earlier more awake state, and the short power nap confused her senses. I take off her shoes, put a blanket over her, and go to the kitchen. There I take out a bottle of water and even find some painkillers. I bring those to the living room and place the bottle on the table, the pills right next to it. She'll surely be happy to find them once she's awake.

I want to leave, but when I reach the hallway, I notice the many framed photos hanging on her walls. London is in most of them and looks happy and lively. The two women appear at different stages of their lives—young girls in school, on a trip to an amusement park. They even went through their emo phase together and later partied often. Smiling, I study one picture more closely: the two of them lying in a meadow with little daisies in their hair. The radiant smile is contagious.

Not bad, Miss Waverley.

If London ever smiled at me like that, I could easily fall in love with her. I stare at the picture longer than I should, then turn away. No. Wait. I take a step back. I want to see it again. Just for one more brief moment.

I pull out my phone and snap a photo of it. I just have to. Only then do I head to the door, take out the key, and place it on the sideboard before leaving Vanessa's apartment.

Well, well. So, London told her how much she hates me? That must have been around the time she threatened to make my life hell.

Three older brothers. I wonder if London will tell me about them if I ask more directly? I'm curious.

I go back downstairs to my car.

That was a really interesting conversation. It's a shame Vanessa was so drunk. A little tipsy would have been enough to get more out of her. But now I know where she lives, and maybe I can pay her a visit sometime if London herself doesn't provide new information.

Sitting in the car, I look at the photo again.

Oh, London. You've just become a lot more intriguing than I ever would have guessed.

And this city isn't as bad as I remembered it five years ago when I moved to New York.

Chapter 11

London

I haul the groceries into my apartment and sort out the little treats Stephanie asked for. Luckily, there are plenty of vegan options these days, so I can offer her more than just an apple or banana. I picked up some yogurt and pudding, chocolate, pralines, different drinks and teas she likes, plus a few dishes I can cook so we'll have enough to eat here. I figure if we cook together and enjoy the meal, we could become good friends. That would be great. After all, Alexander called her his best friend, and I can't afford to mess things up with her a second time.

Me: Got lots of stuff, looking forward to seeing you :)

Stephanie: Well, I'm curious. See you tomorrow :)

Oh, perfect. A smiley!

I head to the bathroom, brush my teeth, and scroll through Vanessa's avalanche of messages while doing so—over fifty. She clearly has too much time and...

But as I skim them, unease pools in my stomach. What is this? She wants to come to the office? Talk to Alexander? My eyes widen in panic, and I call her while rinsing my mouth. It rings and rings but no answer.

Oh God!

I scroll further down and see she texted that she's in a taxi. But that was an hour ago!

Dear God, why? Why me?

I call her again and type at the same time: *Please don't go, I'll handle this!*

Looks like my streak of bad luck isn't over yet. I let it ring and rinse my mouth again. Mope. Still not answering.

"Oh, come on, Nessa! Pick up! Please!"

In a panic, I text Alexander: "*My best friend might show up at the office today. Please just ignore her!*"

Alex: Too late.
Me: What's that supposed to mean?
Alex: She already found me. She took a taxi here, and I drove her home.
Me: Please, PLEASE tell me this is a joke!
Alex: She was a bit tipsy and fell asleep in my car. But I got Vanessa to her apartment and now I'm on my way home. Your friend is really funny.
Me: I'm so sorry!
Alex: No need. She really stood up for you.
Me: She's going through a rough patch right now.
Alex: Yeah, I know the story. I think you told me about five times today.
Me: She gets a little melancholic when she drinks. Please don't hold it against her.
Alex: She talks a lot if you let her :)
Me: What did she tell you?
Alex: Not much.
Me: Come on, tell me!
Alex: Your shift is over. See you tomorrow.
Me: Alex! Answer me!
No reply. Of course.

I sit on the edge of the bathtub, face burning, staring up at the ceiling.

God, are you punishing me? What on earth did I do to deserve this torture?

I sigh, lower my gaze, and try to pull myself together. I call Vanessa a few more times while changing into something comfortable and packing my gym bag. She's probably sleeping the alcohol off. So, I text her: "*What did you tell Alex?*"

Maybe instead of going to the gym, I should hit the boxing ring instead? I haven't been there in weeks.

I check the hours online—still the same. Perfect. I really feel like punching a sandbag. This anger has to go somewhere, and fast.

It takes me only about twenty minutes, even with stop-and-go traffic, to get to the sports hall on the edge of downtown. The building sits off to the side in a quiet area—you wouldn't expect a boxing club here. Mostly young men come here to prove themselves. Women are rare. But I kinda like that.

After parking, I head for the entrance with my bag. The heavy steel door is propped open, letting a little fresh air into the heated interior. I can already smell the sweat even from here.

"Hey," I say to the two musclebound guys at the entrance. They give me a short nod.

"Haven't seen you in a while, Princess," one of them calls out. "You've lost some muscle. Need training help?" He laughs suggestively, and I roll my eyes.

"I need a punching bag," I answer promptly. "Can you take a few kicks and punches, or are you gonna cry if I hit you in the wrong spot?"

He's left speechless while his buddy bursts out laughing.

"Let me know if you really want to help." I smile and head into the locker room.

There's one for women, though I've often been "invited" to change with the men. As long as the boss isn't around, some of the guys act like rats when the cat's away.

After changing, I step into the main room. Three boxing rings, bags hanging from the walls, mats spread out. People are training hard to blasting music. The bass thumps through the floor.

Looks like I'm the only woman here today. Most of the guys just want to burn off energy, and the ones who get a little sassy usually mean well—they're the first to step in if someone needs help. But when they're just with each other, their mouths run nonstop. Still, there's something solid behind all the talk.

I head to an empty corner to train in peace. I set my towel, water bottle, and gloves on the bench, then stretch and warm up before starting with light exercises. A minute with the jump rope, then I slide on my gloves, my fingers peeking through. They fit snugly, the wraps protecting my joints.

After just a few punches, I feel how out of practice I am. That's what I get. It's been at least six weeks, even though I meant to come for an hour once a week. That has to change from now on.

I work the bag hard, and it instantly feels so good to take my frustration out on it.

"What'd it ever do to you?" a male voice says from behind me.

"Are you talking to me?" I ask, still focused on the punching bag. I want to finish my set before taking a break, and he's distracting me.

"Of course. You've got quite a punch. Not bad," he says. Hopefully that's all it is—I'm not here to flirt. "Want me to hold it steady, or..." He steps closer, and my eyes nearly pop out when I see *who* just spoke.

"Alex?" I immediately stop, and he looks just as surprised.

"Uh... or are you going to hit me instead?" he finishes with a laugh. "What are you doing here?"

"I should be asking you that!" He's only wearing a tight muscle shirt, and I can see every line of his toned arms. Damn. Were those hidden under that suit? I force myself to meet his eyes, silently praying he doesn't sneak a glance at my neckline. He'd better not!

"Small world, huh?" He grips the bag with one hand. "I know the owner from way back. He invited me to train here again. I haven't been in London in five years."

I let out a quiet sigh. Great. So, he's not going anywhere anytime soon.

"You know Carlos?" I ask, throwing another punch. Alex holds the bag casually, but his arm keeps flexing. I keep at it until he finally has to use both hands.

"Started coming here when I was seventeen, just to blow off steam. So you're the 'princess' he always talks about, I take it?"

"They call every woman here that. Except Manuela. She's got more muscle than half the guys. She's the queen."

"Alright, Princess. Hit harder, I can barely feel it," he teases. That makes me stop.

"I haven't been here in weeks," I protest, already out of breath.

"Yeah, I can tell. Want to try holding it?" One punch from him and I'd probably fly into the wall.

"Alex, you can't make our princess hold the bag," a deep voice rumbles. I'd know Carlos's voice anywhere.

The massive Greek towers even over Alex by a few inches. He's got more chest hair than I have hair on my head, but his dark, tattooed look is misleading—despite the face tattoos, the thick black bears and all the ink, he's the gentlest of them all.

"I'll hold it."

He plants himself behind the bag like a rock so Alex can punch, while I step aside and try to catch my breath.

That gives me a chance to sneak a look at Alex. Black muscle shirt, athletic shorts, that reveal that even his calves are cut. His punches land precise and powerful. Even Carlos actually struggles to hold the bag. I'd definitely have flown into the nearest wall.

"And she was supposed to hold this? You've still got a hell of a punch, Lex!"

Lex?

"But you can push harder. Really give it all, come on! Harder!"

Alex works up a sweat fast. I bet his muscles are burning already. Veins are pulsing on his arms and sweat soaks through his shirt.

Damn. That looks so good.

"Our little princess here looks impressed!" Carlos calls out, and just like that Alex's eyes meet mine.

Oops.

My face heats, and I quickly step away to calm down, staring at the ceiling. The ceiling fans are blasting, but I'm still hot. "Where'd you train in America?"

"Just the gym," Alex says, backing away and catching his breath.

"I want you here every week now." Carlos turns to me. "And you, Princess, preferably every day."

"I probably can't keep that up," I admit.

"But it makes my guys happy," he chuckles, giving me a light pat on the shoulder that nearly knocks me forward. His gentleness is enough to break a bone. "Like a leaf in the wind. Girl, you need more protein. Treat yourself to a steak tonight. Or two. You're wasting away."

"I let my training slide," I confess.

"You'll get it back." He looks at Alex. "And don't you dare anything of hers."

"Not planning to," Alex says with a grin, and they high-five.

"Got tax paperwork to do. Behave yourselves." Carlos nods and leaves, and suddenly it's just Alex and me again.

"So, you didn't tell him I'm your father's assistant?"

"No. Should I?" He smirks and braces the bag so I can keep punching. Unlike him, though, I'm much slower. Compared to his tree-trunk arms, mine look like twigs.

"I could tell him you were rude to me. He'd flatten you." I grin.

"Fair," he admits with a smile. "Try punching from the shoulder. Full extension. You're holding back."

"I'm totally out of shape," I complain.

"That's why I'm telling you—swing properly and keep moving."

He smiles and I'm actually glad to return it. Okay, this is... nice. Maybe even fun.

I bounce lightly, try to move a bit more, and put more power into the next punch.

"Much better. Again! Come on, keep going!" His voice is firm, commanding. Controlled.

Damn it—it's turning me on. Not now. God, not now. Not him. Not here!

"I need a break," I pant, turning away. Wall. Gray, rough plaster. Yes, focus on the wall. Not his muscles. Bad idea. He's—probably—about to be my new boss. That's what I should be thinking about. Not his strong, well-toned arms and... a wall. Wall! Look at the wall, London!

I close my eyes, and a moment later something soft touches my neck. I open them to find Alex draping my towel over my shoulders.

"Rest up. That wasn't half bad for a beginner." He picks up my water bottle, but instead of handing it to me, he twists the cap open and sniffs it.

"Is this just water?"

"Yes."

"No electrolytes?"

"I was just planning to hit the gym and didn't bring anything else. At the gym you can refill bottles, but here there's just water."

Alex grabs another bottle and a black towel from the bench, wipes his face, then pours some of his drink into mine.

"Let me guess—you only had that fruit for lunch today?"

"And the salad. And the wrap."

He gives me a scolding look. "No protein? No shake? No sports drink? Not even a banana?"

"I didn't have time."

"No wonder you're so weak."

"Hey…" I protest weakly.

"Drink first. I've been here longer. If you want to keep going, fine, but not too much. Not on an empty stomach."

"But I did eat…"

"At lunch. Are you trying to starve yourself? That's not how muscle building works. You'll just lose water, and your body will start eating away at what little it has left—your muscles. You'll gain weight and lose muscle mass," he lectures, then takes a drink from his bottle.

"I know. I just didn't have the headspace for it today. I only came here to hit something."

"Rough day, huh?" he asks, amused.

"You could say that."

"Wouldn't it be something if your boss walked in right now and you could punch him instead?"

"Mr. Blackthorn isn't here, though."

"You could take it out on me, instead," he suggests. His smile is stunning, and of course, I instantly smile back.

Damn. I was trying to keep it together!

"He hasn't done anything to me, but his son…" I trail off, giving him a look.

"The one who invited you to dinner? Yeah, that sounds terrible. Awful boss."

"He's probably fine. I'm just frustrated with myself." Not entirely true, but a solid excuse. I only drink after he nudges the bottom of my bottle with his fingertips, forcing me to put it to my lips.

"Exercise helps with that. But prep is key. I wouldn't want you to burn out."

"Someone's thinking practically."

"I always do. Princess." Of course he calls me that now.

"I think I'll head out. I've only been here about twenty minutes, but that's enough. The frustration's gone."

Desire, on the other hand, is not—and I need an ice-cold shower as soon as possible. The last thing I need is to picture my boss naked.

"What are you doing?" I blurt when Alex strips off his shirt and tosses it on the bench.

"It was just getting in the way." He takes another drink, giving me a perfect view of his toned torso. Every inch is perfectly defined. And those hip bones, those abs that flex with every slight movement...

I whip my eyes away and finish my bottle.

"Yeah, so... I'll be going home now to throw a steak in the pan," I announce.

"Don't you want to ask me about your best friend?" he tempts, making me freeze.

"I completely forgot!"

"Not enough electrolytes," he jokes with a grin.

"What did she tell you? About my brothers?"

"That you have three. Older ones. Then she fell asleep."

"Nothing else?"

"She apologized. Put you in a good light."

"Anything else?"

"No."

"Then why are you grinning like that?"

"Oh, I think I'll keep that to myself." Smiling broadly, he turns away, sets his bottle down, and gets back to the punching bag like nothing happened. He looks stunning even from behind.

"Okay, I'm really leaving now!"

No, I shouldn't be staring at his back or his firm ass. Or those muscular calves.

Bad. Stop. Shame on me.

I should be ashamed of myself. Totally ashamed.

"See you tomorrow," he calls, still punching while I head out.

Better hurry.

I grab my stuff and rush to the locker room, and shower as quickly as humanly possible.

One ice-cold shower later, I stand in front of the locker room mirror. My cheeks are still bright red, like I just ran a marathon in 104-degree heat. I sigh, patting my neck dry. The cold droplets feel soothing. I drink more water, then slump onto the bench, sigh loudly, and dig my phone out of my pocket. Still nothing from Nessa, of course. I'd love to call and wake her up, but she should probably sleep off her hangover.

I finally go through her messages in peace. She went to the doctor and got a two-week sick leave so she wouldn't have to show up at school with swollen eyes from crying. I get that all too well. If it had been me, I'd feel the same.

I type back: *Hey, I talked to Alex. Everything's fine. But please—no more spontaneous stunts, okay? Especially not after drinking. Better yet, stay away from alcohol altogether, alright? Hugs.*

I get dressed, leave the studio, and head home—already planning to cook myself something good to eat. Next time, And next time before I go training, I'll prepare myself better.

Chapter 12

Alexander

I kind of had hoped my physique might impress her. Hard to believe she actually works out here.

"So, you know her?" Carlos leans back in his office chair while I—freshly showered and changed—sit across from him with a protein shake while he flips through paperwork.

"She's my father's PA," I explain briefly. "But he's stepping down Friday, and I'm taking over. She'll be assigned to me then."

"Lucky you. That girl's turned down everyone here. Even Leonardo. And no one says no to him."

I perk up at that.

"She looks amazing, has a killer figure, and she's quick-witted. And she'll be working under you? If I were in your position, I know what I'd do with her." He grins and clarifies: "I mean, if I wasn't married, didn't have five wonderful kids, and was twenty years younger. Then definitely."

"Right. But I'm definitely not getting involved with employees. That's messy. That always ends badly."

"Still such a decent guy, Lex." He chuckles and slides a sleek black card with gold lettering across the desk. "Ever heard of these guys?"

I pick it up and examine it more closely. "MG?"

There's a coat of arms divided into four. A lion in the upper left quarter, a fleur-de-lis in the lower right, which actually comes from French heraldry. Upper right has the M and lower left the G. "What does it stand for?"

"Millionaires and Gentlemen's Club," Carlos says, putting away a file. "Some of our members are in it. When they heard you'd be training here, they asked me to give you that invitation."

"Exclusive club, then?"

"Very. Only filthy rich guys with manners. Not just money—but brains too." He taps his temple. "You'd fit right in, no?"

"So, it's a men's club. And they gave this to you?"

"I'm a trustworthy man."

"They paid you to pitch it, didn't they?" I ask the old warrior.

"No, but I know several of them well. One told me they'd selected you."

"So not his call."

"Apparently not."

I flip the card over. "Coordinates," I murmur.

"Though that was a phone number."

"I'll check it out. No harm in looking." I nod at him. "Heading home now. If it's nearby, I might stop by tonight."

"Put in a good word for me, maybe they'll let me in too," he laughs.

"If not you, then who?" We stand, shake hands, and I grab my bag. It's just before ten. Time enough for a small detour.

In my car, I enter the coordinates. The address is right in the middle of downtown. I take a closer look and realize it's a hotel. The MG. How fitting, though it actually stands for Montgomery Grey—a real estate guy who died a year ago. He owned half of England, or so it felt. His family split the property empire. One of them must have taken over the hotel and decided to open a club there. Interesting.

I'm about to put my phone away but hesitate. I want to look at London's picture again. Her smile lingers in my head, impossible to shake.

Fifteen minutes later, I pull into the hotel's valet service and my car disappears underground while I step into a lobby. Elegant men and women are mingling. A single night here costs five hundred pounds at least. Regular tourists rarely wander in here.

At the reception desk, a pretty blonde beams at me. The second I slide the card across, she knows exactly what to do.

"Welcome, Mr. Blackthorn. Thank you for accepting our invitation. May I ask you to follow me?"

"Gladly."

She clicks away on her heels, and I follow her to an elevator with a red carpet and its own attendant. A young brunette takes over now. "Welcome, Mr. Blackthorn," she chirps as well. "You're already expected."

"I'm quite curious," I say as she presses the button and shortly after, the elevator doors open. Both ladies accompany me. They select the top floor—then we zip upward.

When we arrive, the doors open again and both ladies step forward. However, the blonde stays by the elevator while the brunette takes me with her. I only see the blonde bow before heading back down.

The anteroom is luxurious—Appealing art and elaborately designed plants welcome me. Only the finest materials have been used in the floor, walls, and ceiling. There's even a small fountain that gently bubbles away. The room is bathed in a pleasantly warm light, creating a cozy ambiance that seems slightly dim yet erotic to me.

We reach a black double door, and she opens it. Soft piano music drifts out immediately, and the scent of alcohol wafts to my nose.

I follow her into a massive, labyrinth-like room. Besides pure luxury, there's also a huge aquarium filled with exotic fish. It takes up an entire wall, though you can still see clearly through to the other side. There are also terrariums with trees and plants—but no animals. They stretch from the floor up to the ceiling, nearly twenty feet high.

I spot a pianist playing at a white grand piano. The entire penthouse suite is surrounded by glass walls, offering a perfect view of London. The countless city lights look like a night sky of their own—which sadly can't be admired. London is too bright, even in the dead of night.

I keep following the lady. Here and there are a few men around my age, being served food and drinks by pretty, scantily clad women. Quiet conversations take place, while others entertain themselves at the billiard table.

She leads me toward a group of four men. Among them, I notice Montgomery Grey's grandson, Cornelius Grey. With dark brown hair, he doesn't really stand out from the group. Only the gold ring with the MG crest catches my eye. The gazes of his three conversation partners—whom I can't place right away—shift toward me, which makes him turn around.

"Alexander Blackthorn," he says warmly, waving over one of the servers. She hurries over immediately with a tray of whiskey glasses balanced neatly in her hands. He takes two of them and hands me one, while the brunette withdraws and disappears from view. "So, you accepted my invitation."

"I just followed the coordinates Carlos gave me." I study his face, trying to read him, though it's hard in such a place with alcohol and several young women.

"When I heard you were back in London, I had to send for you." His smile is brief. How old is he? Early or mid-thirties, maybe? It's hard to say. He gestures to the three men scrutinizing me nearby. "Allow me to introduce you."

I observe the three watching me with curiosity.

"This is Alexander Blackthorn, only son of Arthur Blackthorn."

At my father's name, recognition flickers. One by one Cornelius introduces me to the men who are there. All of them heirs of English, French, or American dynasties. There's even a Swiss heir among them, though most of them are English. We stroll around and chat a little before we're alone after the brief tour.

On the terrace outside, models lounge around and inside a roofed pool.

"I see, you've built yourself quite a little paradise," I remark. Cornelius is almost done with his whiskey, while mine is mostly untouched.

"That's just for show. The ladies are off-limits. Relationships with them aren't tolerated—they're here to attend to every gentleman here, not one man in particular." He grins and adds, "Although, it can be... entertaining to break the occasional taboo now and then."

Of course.

"So what's the purpose of this club?"

"Business. Connections. Good food. Good drinks." He nods at my whiskey. "We have wine too, if that's more your style."

"I still have to drive."

"We're open from six pm to three in the morning, seven days a week. Someone is always here. I spend most of my time enjoying life. But you can also come and use one of the offices. We also have suites prepared below in case you'd rather leave in the morning." His smile tilts, sly. "And if you'd rather not sleep alone—I keep a list of beautiful women who'd definitely appeal to you."

"Got it." I drain my glass and moment later, a young lady rushes over to get my glass. I decline a refill.

Well, I should be going. But I can see myself dropping by on occasion."

Cornelius clasps my hand in a strong, commanding shake. Right now, he's one of the most influential and wealthy men in all of England and having someone like that as a business partner definitely has its advantages.

Chapter 13

London

London

I don't open Vanessa's late-night messages until the next morning. By then I'd already been fast asleep.

I'm still in bed as I read what she texted me: "*I was completely wasted. God, I can barely remember anything. Just that he was really polite and respectful, and brought me to my apartment and well, that was it. He even tucked me in! And he left a bottle of water on the table—he even thought of painkillers!*

I won't touch another drop. Promise. I'm just going to find a new man. A really sweet, great, kind and faithful guy who I can shower with my love. I'll never let an idiot like Dominic into my life again!"

Well, I certainly hope so.

I get ready for the day and leave early. Mornings are lovely when you're freshly showered and pumped full of coffee. It really wakes you up.

By the time I arrive at the office, I'm actually excited to start the day. Alexander will be busy, and Mr. Blackthorn has a long list he wants to work through, which means I can focus on planning the party in peace.

Twenty minutes later, Alexander strides in, heading straight for my desk and nods at me amiably.

"So? Did you eat your steak yesterday?"

"Yes and woke up with aching muscles. My neck's so tense."

"You should book a massage. Convenient to have one right in the building."

"Every slot's taken. It'll ease up eventually. Consider it punishment for rarely working out—especially with a substitute trainer who encouraged me to hit harder." I shoot him a half-reproachful look before smiling.

Okay, I might actually have a good time with him as my boss.

"I do what I can," he says, then asks. "So—are you looking forward to tonight?"

Stephanie must have told him.

"Yes. We're cooking something vegan and chatting a bit. I'm hoping to pry some of your dark secrets out of her." If he's pumped Vanessa for information, I'll try and get as much as possible from Stephanie.

"She knows pretty much everything. The question is what you'll do with the info." Alexander watches me fascinated. It seems he feels challenged. Does he think this some kind of game?

"I'm sure opportunities will present themselves," I reply mysteriously, before turning to my computer. "I should get to work."

"So, should I fetch my own coffee?"

"I'll bring it right away..."

This guy.

"Much obliged." He grins before retreating to his office, while I save the email. Shortly after I go get the esteemed gentleman his coffee.

The rest of the day goes by without a hitch. Alexander is even having lunch with his father, leaving me to enjoy my break alone. I really only see him and Mr. Blackthorn when refilling their coffee or ushering department heads to Alexander for their meetings.

I want to leave on time, so I head to Mr. Blackthorn's office. Alexander is there too.

"Do you need anything else?" I ask my boss.

"No, feel free to go home, Miss Waverley. We'll see you tomorrow."

Since I know him well, I linger.

"Oh, there is one more thing."

Yep, that's what I thought.

"How's the planning coming along?"

"Very well," I assure him. "But that's all you'll get out of me. It's meant to be a surprise."

Day two, successfully completed, I'd say.

"Then have a pleasant evening, Miss Waverley," he says, while Alexander just gives me a silent nod.

"You too. Both of you."

I close the door behind me, however, I'm curious and linger a moment to listen. Normally, I'd never eavesdrop. But after yesterday with Alexander, today's uneventfulness feels... unsettling. And Mr. Blackthorn's office door is considerably thinner, and I can easily listen in on what they're saying.

"Well? Are you satisfied with her?" my boss asks.

See? Knew it. Good thing I stayed.

"To be honest, yes. She does her job and doesn't get on my nerves."

Well, not exactly glowing praise, Alexander.

My boss laughs. "I can see it written all over your face. You like her. Admit it. You have my blessing."

"Father!"

"You won't find anyone better. Ask her out."

Oh my goodness! My eyes widen my eyes and my breath catches for a moment.

"I just want to work with her. There's enough to do. I'm taking over the company on Monday after all."

"I'll still be around for a few months—as advisor and board member. At least until Christmas. But I'll be scaling back my hours significantly and will only come in on occasion. You can move into my office then."

"I prefer the other one. You can keep this one, if for nostalgia's sake."

"Shall I introduce you to someone else, if Miss Waverley isn't to your taste?"

"I'll find someone myself."

Okay. I should go. I slip away, careful not to let my heels click against the floor—that would be way too loud. I quickly take my cup and water glass in the kitchen, shut down my computer, and grab my things. I want to get home as early as possible so there's enough time to welcome Stephanie.

But as I drive home, I start thinking.

I'm not Alexander's type?

After the boxing club last night, I could've sworn he was flirting a little. That's my worst fear: I find him hot, but he doesn't reciprocate the feeling. That could become a problem. I absolutely can't develop a crush on him.

At home, I wipe down the kitchen surfaces one last time. The doorbell rings. I buzz Stephanie in and tell her to take the elevator through the intercom. Moments later, she's at my door.

There she is: long blonde hair that's slightly curly and perfectly made up. She has full lips and steel-blue eyes, as well as a perfect figure. Large breasts, a snatched waist with a blessed bubble butt. She's wearing a mini skirt and a dark blue blouse, high heels and also freshly manicured nails.

Wow, what a dream girl!

I admit I'm a little intimidated. So this is Alexander's childhood best friend. I swallow.

"Hey!" I beam at Stephanie and simply hug her. She smells wonderful—like flowers, and her hands rest gently like butterfly wings on my back. "Did you find your way here easily?"

I pull away from her and invite her in. She's only carrying a small handbag that hangs loosely over her shoulder.

"Yes, thank you. Your directions were perfect." She seems a bit shy, but also curious and critical. It's obvious she doesn't trust me yet.

"Let me show you around first, then maybe we can cook something together? I bought some stuff. Vegan, of course."

"I'd like that."

I close the door behind her. "So this is my hallway. You can leave your shoes here—there's a small storage closet." I keep walking while she slips off her heels. "This is the living room—it's small but nice." I've got a couch for two, a comfy reading chair, and a TV on the wall. The kitchen is open, so I can run the coffee maker while standing in the hallway. Between the hallway and the living room, a narrow corridor leads to my bedroom and the bathroom. "The bathroom even has a window. The bedroom's also pretty compact." Only a bed fits in there, but I'm glad I found an apartment with a separate bedroom at all.

"I thought you earned good money?" she asks, surprised. "I don't mean to be rude, but can't you afford something much bigger?"

"Yes, it's only about 440 square feet, but it's in a good part of town. Right now I'm paying £2,200 in rent, utilities included. That's already quite a bit." London has gotten incredibly expensive over the past few years. "I've got about £5,300 left after taxes. I save for hard times. The car is also costly. Plus, I've got a few private insurance policies and well..."

"I get it. I'll kindly point out to Alexander that he should pay you a bit more. A PA should live appropriately." She winks at me. "*His* PA should be living in style." I don't take it as criticism—just take the opportunity to smile back at her.

"I've got no objections to that." We both laugh as I lead her back to the living room. "Tea?"

"I'd love some."

"I bought the peppermint tea you like so much." Even the brand she mentioned. It wasn't easy to find, but I wanted to make a good impression. "And all the ingredients for a vegan lasagna."

"Well then, let's cook," she suggests.

Perfect. That way we'll both have something to do instead of just staring at each other while chatting. I hand her a flower-print apron while I take my pink one.

"You must have a lot of questions about me showing up at the church?"

"Yes, though Marc already told me quite a bit. Alex too. But I'd like to hear your version. Honestly, I'm still not fully convinced your friend wasn't having an affair with Marc..."

"Actually, I can put your mind at ease about that. The idiot's name is Dominic, and he got married on the same day. I even found the wedding announcement." It's lying on the table. "He's forty-one and works as a banker here in London. Nessa and he—well, that's short for Vanessa—Um, they met only a few weeks ago. I was really happy for her but only knew him from her stories. She said he's shy, didn't have much time, and wanted to get to know her discreetly before meeting family or friends. Honestly, I found that strange. After all, he works at a bank. How can someone be shy in that profession?"

I sigh and start taking the ingredients out of the fridge and my shopping basket. "But she'd been single for so long and seemed happy, so I kept my mouth shut. Well, until the drama started and she found out he was getting married. Then I was furious immediately. How dare this jerk treat my best friend like that? So, I said, 'We're going there now and crashing that wedding.'"

I snort angrily and slam the vegan ground meat onto the counter, then wash my hands. Stephanie does the same.

"But Nessa was afraid to face him, so she sent me to the wrong address. She didn't know there was another wedding happening there. She was completely intimidated and well... then chaos commenced blew up. You know the rest."

"And Marc doesn't know her?"

"No. I didn't know him either. And finding out Alex would be my new boss really threw me. When he showed up at the office on Monday, I told security not to let him in."

"You're kidding." Stephanie laughs and dries her hands.

"No, I'm serious. I thought he had tracked me down. I panicked..."

"Yes, he said he was totally surprised to see you there. What a crazy coincidence." Stephanie glances at the newspaper, which I find a little odd. "So, there isn't a single photo of your friend with Dominic?"

"She secretly took a few pictures of him. I still have them." I point to my phone. "Go ahead, open Nessa's chat. Just look at the last few pictures she sent me."

Letting her snoop through that chat is me showing trust. I don't have anything to hide anyway.

"Really?"

"Of course." I start opening packages and pulling out pots and pans. "This'll be my first vegan lasagna. I'm curious how it'll turn out." I glance briefly at Stephanie, who's on my phone.

"There are great substitutes these days. They taste almost like the real thing."

"How long have you been vegan?"

"About a year. It works for me. I don't force it on anyone, though. Marc loves his meat, and I'd never forbid him that."

"Did you find the pictures?"

"Mmh, yeah..."

I leave her to it and focus on the recipe I printed out beforehand. "Are you getting along with Alex?" she asks while still looking through my phone.

"Not at first. But I think it'll be fine. He's a good guy—we just got off on the wrong foot."

"Are you single, by the way?"

"Yes. For ages," I admit sheepishly. "My last relationship was three years ago. He wanted marriage, kids, a little house on the edge of London, and I was supposed to play housewife. But I wanted my career and didn't want to depend on a man. Now I regret it. I mean, I love my job, but back then I thought family could wait. And now that's exactly what I want." I sigh softly, then glance at her inquisitively. "It's strange how we long for what we could've had but didn't appreciate at the time. If I could go back, I would've said yes. I'd probably be a mother by now." I sigh quietly.

"I know what you mean. I resisted marriage for a long time too. But when I met Marc..." She trails off, absorbed in my phone, I assume she's reading through more of my chat with Nessa.

I let her be. It's only the last three months, anyway, and I deleted the worst bits during my lunch break.

"So you want kids too?" I ask.

"Mmh, yes... with the right man." She looks up at me and smiles. "Which I now have."

"Yeah. I hope I'll be that lucky someday. I just need to find the right one now."

"Alex's not your type?"

I half-expected her to keep asking about Nessa, but instead she redirects everything back to Alex. I suspect he's asked her to pump me for information. Better to play it safe and paint him as a kind and great person.

"No, not at all. I like men with a little belly. Blond with glasses would be perfect. If you know anyone like that, send him my way."

"You don't find Alex attractive?"

"He's a handsome man, sure. But no, definitely not. He's not my type at all."

Her expression doesn't change, but she nods.

"Not what you expected to hear?" I press.

"Women usually go crazy when they see him. He's basically every woman's dream man." She looks at me and smiles. "We're probably the only two people on this planet who don't find him hot."

"Seems so." We both laugh. Stephanie moves closer to help me with the cooking, and I feel like she's finally starting to open up.

"Be honest," I say. "How often have your friends asked you to set them up with him?"

She rolls her eyes. "All the time. Literally every single one of them. Even the ones already in relationships. Of course, it's mostly because of his looks. But he's also got a good character, money, influence, intelligence... It's like God gave him all the things most men are missing."

"Money is always nice, sure but I find wit and charm way more interesting."

"True." Stephanie smiles. "Marc is like that. He always makes me laugh. When I'm near him, I feel at home. And when he's gone—especially for longer stretches—I feel like I'm not really living."

"Is he away often?"

"Hm?" She looks at me, puzzled.

"Marc. I don't even know what your husband does for a living. Does he also run a company like Alex?"

"Yes. Alex gave him money to start his own business. Basically, it's similar to what Alex does—some kind of tech, programs, computer stuff. I don't really get it."

"Honestly? I don't either," I admit. "As a PA, I make coffee, organize documents, schedule appointments... I couldn't even begin to explain to anyone what we sell. But I always know where my boss is and who he's meeting." I giggle.

"Do you enjoy your work?"

"Absolutely. I have my own domain, my peace and quiet, and I can plan. I love planning things." Then, curious, I ask, "What about you?"

"I don't work. I'm a... professional daughter, so to speak." She doesn't seem the least bit bothered by that. "But I studied history because I found it fascinating. My parents own real estate, which I'll probably inherit or manage one day. We'll see... For now, I just want to focus on being a good wife."

Wow. I never thought I'd meet someone like this in real life.

"There's plenty to do in that role," I say.

"The house is big, I exercise a lot, and I make sure Marc always has something good to eat."

But isn't she bored? Whatever. That's none of my business.

"Do you enjoy cooking?"

"Yes, I love it. When you asked if I wanted to cook with you, I instantly liked you." She beams as she stirs the béchamel sauce: vegan butter, flour, plant milk, nutritional yeast, salt, pepper, and nutmeg. I'm really curious how it'll taste.

Meanwhile, I'm frying the vegan ground meat, chopping an onion, and mixing it in with the carrots before gradually adding the rest.

We chat a bit more—about the dreary London weather, current movies and shows—while layering the lasagna and sliding it into the oven. Afterward, we pour tea and make ourselves comfortable on the couch.

"How did you meet Alex?" I ask.

"In school. My parents are from France, and we moved to London when I was eleven. I already spoke fluent English, so school wasn't hard. It was this elite private school with uniforms—really fancy. I liked that." She looks dreamy and nostalgic. I sip my tea as she goes on. "At first, I was the total outsider. The new girl. The weird one from enemy France."

"It's crazy that there's still resentment after all these years," I say. "The war was ages ago."

"Yeah..." She sighs, then continues, "Alex was in my class, but I never really noticed him. Three years later, I still had no friends and was being bullied, he eventually caught on. The mean girls in my class were always cruel in secret, so no one ever noticed. Not even Alex. He thought they were my friends. For a while, I did too, until I realized they were just mocking me." She smiles. "Then one day Alex caught them hitting me."

"What?" I'm horrified. Even girls can be really nasty and disgusting. And at a young age!

"I always thought if I endured it long enough, they'd eventually lose interest. But it only got worse. Alex saw it and put them in their place. He gave them such a scolding they never dared touch me again." Stephanie beams and looks at me, delighted. "He was my hero. That's how we became best friends."

"Alex, the noble knight. And then he even set you up. Has he known Marc for that long too?"

"Yeah, but only since college. They were taking the same course. I went to a different university because I wasn't interested in economics. He and Marc did a lot together. Eventually, we always hung out as a trio. At first, I wasn't really interested in Marc, but he fell in love with me from our first meeting."

"And when did you finally give him a chance?"

"The spark happened only six months ago. He had started dating other women, and I saw how poorly they treated him. Alex was in the U.S. at the time, so I tried to be a better friend to Marc. So I cheered him up. Told him what a fantastic guy he was, and that a woman would be stupid not to appreciate him. He asked me if I was stupid too. That's when it clicked. I always thought he just had a crush, but it was real love from the very beginning. How could I not want to marry him?"

"Wow. He held on for a long time." I let out a deep breath. "And then I ruined your wedding."

Now I feel even worse than before.

"I think from today on we can laugh about it. At least it makes for an exciting story to tell our kids someday."

"True." We giggle and keep chatting until the lasagna is ready and we can try it. And I have to admit—it tastes almost exactly like the real thing. If I didn't know better, I'd never guess the meat and cheese weren't made from cow's milk.

Stephanie and I talk a little longer before she glances at the clock.

"It's already nine. I really need to head home—our flight leaves tomorrow evening."

"Where to?"

"Two weeks in Zanzibar."

"Wow, that sounds amazing. Do you like flying?"

"We're taking my father's jet. That definitely makes it easier."

"I hope with a lockable sleeping area?" I tease as I walk her to the door.

"Oh, yeah..." She laughs, then suddenly pulls me into her arms. "London, it was so lovely meeting you. I hope we can do this again when I'm back?"

"Absolutely." Maybe I've just found a new friend. That would be wonderful.

When I'm alone again, I call Nessa. I'd texted her earlier that I couldn't talk, but she still tried.

"Hey," I greet her, stretching out my legs.

"Finally," she says, almost desperate. "Is she gone?"

"Yeah. It went really well, actually. She asked me a million questions, but Stephanie's genuinely very sweet. We clicked well."

"So, she's not mad anymore?"

"No, everything's fine." I can hear Vanessa taking a deep breath. She seems just as relieved as I am. "Honestly, I never thought she'd handle it so calmly. In her shoes, I might've strangled me. I mean, I almost ruined her wedding. Well... I did, kinda."

"She doesn't sound like the grudge-holding type. Lucky you."

Very lucky, indeed.

I can't help a yawn. "I'm heading to bed. Today wore me out."

"Okay. I won't be doing much more tonight either. I'm going to use the next few days to meditate, then I'll declutter my apartment. I think that will help."

"You need help?"

"Nah, I'll do it on my own. It's my little spring cleaning. I want a fresh start."

"If you need anything, call me, okay? Or text me."

"I will. Talk to you later."

"Sleep well, my little Nessa."

"You too."
We hang up, and I slip into bed, curious what tomorrow will bring.

Chapter 14

Alexander

Alexander

Stephanie texts asking if I have time to talk. I'm in the kitchen preparing a protein shake before bed. I wanna get to bed early tonight. A whole day of meetings with the department heads has drained me, and I'd rather be focused on my US branch—and finally telling the team I'm planning on bringing them to London.

I shake my dinner thoroughly and videocall her. To my surprise, she answers immediately, smiling at the camera in minimal clothing.

"Am I interrupting?" I asked, taken aback.

"No, I'm just doing yoga." She backs up, showing her private home gym. She looks good in her tight leggings and an equally form-fitting top. "What about you? No workout today?"

"Tomorrow." I keep shaking until the powder dissolves. "So? Tell me."

"London's really nice. I believe her. She even let me scroll through her phone. I skimmed her chats with her best friend—there were photos of that Dominic guy. She definitely never had anything with Marc."

"I'm glad. Now you can fly off on your honeymoon tomorrow without worries." I set the shaker down so the foam settles and lean against the counter, watching her exercise.

"Are you considering taking up yoga?" she asks.

"No." Absolutely not. I can't help smiling. Women might look good doing all those poses, but I'll stick to jogging and weights.

"Any news from your housekeeper?"

"No."

"So talkative tonight. Am I distracting you?"

"Just thinking." I just can't get the image of London out of my head. "What kind of person do you think she is?"

"London?"

I nod.

"I think she'd defend her friends to death. But underneath, a genuinely good person. I'm even thinking of setting her up with a friend of mine."

"Why? Is she looking?"

That bothers me. But what bothers me even more is this feeling that I don't want London to date someone.

"I asked if she was into you. She said no. Then she described her type. You're the exact opposite."

"Oh?"

That's even worse.

"Blond. Glasses. Dad bod. Her words." Stephanie bends forward, letting out a brief groan. Then she tosses her blonde hair back while I pick up my shaker, open it, and drink almost all fourteen ounces in one gulp.

"That's her dream man?"

"Yep. I'm thinking of Thomas, what do you think? You've met him, right?"

"That guy? Isn't he over forty?"

"Forty-one. Wealthy, and has been single forever. I think they'd be a great match."

"He sits behind a desk all day. London's a fitness nut. I don't see it."

"I'll still give her his number. I'm good at matchmaking. I know what men want." She kneels in front of the camera and winks at me.

"Or maybe she was just being polite," I mutter. "I am her boss. And you're my best friend."

"Hmm. Maybe." She sighs, fanning herself. "Whew, I'm hot. I'm going for a swim."

"You do that. I'll email the team to tell them I wanna talk later. Maybe I'll even call them instead, so I can get it over with."

"Hey, London is a gorgeous city. I mean… Didn't you miss me at all?"

"Of course I missed you and Marc. But the city itself… not so much. Once you've lived in New York, London seems like… a village."

"London has plenty to offer."

"Yes, she does…" I murmur.

"A beautiful skyline, good restaurants, the royals. Don't forget those."

Right. The city. And yet the only image in my head is her—with flowers in her hair.

"True."

"How about lunch tomorrow? Marc will still be at the company finalizing details before we fly out, but I'll have some time."

"That's pretty short notice."

"Hey, I want to see you once more before I'm gone for two weeks."

"I only have half an hour at most," I say. I actually wanted to eat with London on the roof again, but I can't leave Stephanie hanging.

"I'll take it."

"Okay, are you coming to the office?"

"Yes, I'll bring something, and we can eat there."

"Perfect. See you tomorrow."

"You want to hang up already?"

"Yeah, weren't you going for a swim?"

"Yeah, I was... um, so until tomorrow. One works?"

"Sure, that works."

"Good. See you tomorrow."

I nod to her and hang up. It's best if I talk to the team right now. The sooner everyone knows, the longer they'll have to think it over.

The next morning, I drive to the office again. I park, turn off the engine, and check the messages on my phone again.

So far, only one person from the team has said no. His wife and kids insist on staying in New York. We still need to discuss the severance package, but of course I'll pay him generously. I hope the rest will follow me to London. I need the team on-site—preferably all of them. So, I write back: "Relocation costs will be covered. Housing will also be fully reimbursed. Your children's schooling will be taken care of. Maybe it could be a new beginning?" I completely understand not wanting to uproot their whole life. Even I found it hard to return to London, even though I was born here and was only in New York for five years.

Stephanie has sent me a series of pictures. I just skim through them quickly. Her in yoga clothes. Her in a bikini. Her cooking dinner. Looks like she's missed me. Back in New York, she didn't send that many pictures. She also writes: #perfectwify.

Yes, she is. I text her back a smiley face.

I grab my things and head inside. There's still a lot of work waiting for me today, but I'm really looking forward to seeing London again.

My father is to blame. He planted this idea in my head, and now I can't stop thinking about asking her out.

When I get upstairs, London is already at her desk. She yawns and peers sleepily into her coffee cup.

"Rough night?" I ask, amused. London jumps—she didn't see me coming in. Her cheeks immediately flush. Cute.

"Good morning. Yeah. I couldn't really sleep. But coffee should fix it."

"Still sore from boxing?"

"A little." She rubs her neck.

Should I offer to give her a massage? No, that would be too much. Or would it?

"If I call downstairs, you'll get an appointment right away."

"That wouldn't be fair," she says, which makes me smile.

"I could…" No. I shouldn't offer that. "Well, we could hire someone new. Seems like there's a demand."

"Hmm, I like that. Should I make a job posting?"

"Yes. Starting immediately. You can book an appointment right away or have a trial massage. During working hours, of course."

Yep, that's better than offering to do it myself.

"Well, I'm all for that," she says brightly. "I'll take care of it right away." Seeing her smile feels good.

"Excellent." I'm about to leave but turn back: "Oh, by the way, Stephanie's coming at one. I'll have lunch with her in my office."

"Got it. For an hour?"

"Thirty minutes should be enough."

She looks at her screen. "Your next appointment isn't until 2:30. Technically, she could stay for ninety minutes."

"What happened to the 2 PM appointment?"

"Called in sick. Sports injury. Twisted his ankle playing tennis, but he wants to be back Monday."

"I see." I nod gratefully and turn to leave. But this time, she stops me.

"Has your cleaning lady gotten in touch?"

"No. Unfortunately not yet. I've called her twice—nothing. All the ads she had online for more work have disappeared. I'm afraid she's not coming back."

"I might know someone. She's reliable and dedicated," she says.

"If you recommend her, gladly. Just one thing," I say, looking serious enough that London briefly looks intimidated. "She shouldn't be impulsive. I prefer calm people around me. Unless it's in sports."

"She's the definition of calm."

"Perfect. If my housekeeper doesn't show up Saturday, feel free to send your friend to me."

"Can I get your address?"

"I'll text it to you."

"And, um, what time?"

"Around eleven? She usually comes at ten, so an extra hour should be enough."

London nods and goes back to her computer.

"I'll take care of everything."

"Including coffee?"

She smiles at that. That's better. No more death glares at me.

"I'll bring it in a minute. I turned on the machine earlier but you're twenty minutes early."

"Sounds good, Miss Waverley."

"Always a pleasure, Mr. Blackthorn," she jokes back.

We both smile. But now I really leave and head into my office. A lot of work is waiting today.

At exactly 1:00, there's a knock at the door. I'd been lost in thought and forgot Stephanie was coming. She just walks in before I can even respond.

"Hey. Right on time," I say, standing up. In the background, I see London, who must have walked her up.

"I'll take my break now," I hear her say.

"Enjoy," I reply, then turn to Stephanie, who's armed with two large paper bags.

"Hey," she greets me. We hug warmly while London closes the door.

"Did you get here okay?"

"Yes. Wow, your office looks amazing. Not bad at all." She sets down the two bags and walks over to the windows. "This is the way to work. Such a wonderful view. You can even see Big Ben from here."

"Yes, but I still have to work," I say with a smile.

Stephanie trails a giant cloud of perfume behind her—something like honey, floral, and coconutty. Like she bathed in it. With her white skirt and soft pink blouse, she looks girlish, playfully feminine. "What treats did you bring?"

"You must be starving," she says as she comes closer. She spreads out the food: classic American stuff—burgers, fries, donuts, and sandwiches.

"Oh, wow," I marvel at the spread, laughing. Pretty much the opposite of what I usually eat.

"I figured since you miss the States so much you'd appreciate this."

She looks so excited I can't really say no.

"But you'll eat something too, right?"

"Of course!" she says brightly, glancing around. "Eat over there?"

"Sure." The table's pretty low, but it'll do. We sit down. It's okay to indulge once in a while

"Are you seeing anyone?" she asks as I pick up a burger. At least it's stacked with plenty of meat.

"You mean a woman? No, not right now. I wanted to settle into London first."

Okay, let's taste this. Oh yeah—it's good. Lots of onions, juicy meat, fresh tomato, crisp lettuce. I haven't had anything like this in ages.

"Sometimes the good things are right within reach," she says, raising her eyebrows.

"Are you trying to set me up with London?"

"What?" she asks, irritated.

"My father already wanted me to go out with her."

"And you don't want to?"

"No, she's my... well, she'll soon be my PA, and that's how it should stay. It wouldn't be good." I look at her and add, "Besides, you said she's not into me."

"So, you would go out with her if she was?"

"No. I wouldn't."

"Oh, good."

"Yeah?"

"Yeah. That really only causes trouble," she says firmly.

"True."

"So, what's your dream woman like? I mean, take me as an example—you never asked me out either."

I can't help laughing. "That's because you're like a little sister to me." Still, it's a good question. "Honestly, I don't think I'm made for relationships. Any woman's better off only spending one night with me—nothing more. I don't want to break anyone's heart."

"Being an eternal bachelor isn't exactly ideal either, huh?"

"I just haven't met the right one yet." And I really shouldn't even be thinking about London. I need to shut down those little fantasies as fast as possible.

"What if you already have?" My ears perk up while Stephanie only nibbles on some fries.

"What do you mean?"

"I knew Marc for years before I gave him a chance, and now..." She trails off. "What if there's a woman in your life you just don't notice?"

"Then fate probably doesn't want us together."

"Don't you have any fantasies? Come on. Tell me."

"Hm, she should be smart. Driven. Have that certain spark. Be athletic and know something about nutrition." I glance at my burger and take another bite anyway, even though it's wrecking my whole metabolism.

"The burger wasn't such a good idea, was it?"

"No, it's fine. It's okay to indulge once in a while."

"I usually watch what I eat."

"That's true. You're a role model, really. Even if I can't get on board with all the vegan stuff."

"And I'm athletic too."

"Yeah, you've always been active."

"She'll come along someday, Alex. She's out there. I know it. You just need to open your eyes." Stephanie smiles at me affectionately.

"Thanks. You really are the best little substitute sister I could ask for."

"Yeah, that's absolutely true."

I'm glad she and Marc found each other, even though I was shocked when they got together eventually. After all that time, love still developed between them. I definitely hadn't seen that coming.

We chat about everything until my time's up and soon my next appointment will be in my office.

"Whenever I'm with you, time flies," she says, wrapping her arms around me. I pat her back gently, but she won't let go. "I'm so glad you're finally back here. Promise me you'll never go back to New York, okay? I don't ever want to miss you again."

"I can't promise, but for now it looks like I'm staying."

"Music to my ears."

Stephanie pulls back and looks at me intently before placing her hand on my cheek. "I'll be back in two weeks. Can you even manage without me?"

"I'll try," I tell her. I hadn't realized just how clingy she's been the past few days. She was practically glued to me before the wedding too. She must've really missed me.

After she leaves, I have to air out the office immediately—partly because of her perfume, partly because of the fast-food smell.

There's a knock. My appointment already? Way too early.

"Come in," I call out loudly, otherwise they might not hear me. But it's London, peeking in.

"Hey, do you have a moment? It's about... uh." She hesitates, wrinkling her nose.

"What's worse, perfume or fast food?" I ask.

"The combination. Wow." London coughs and steps back. Then she feels along the wall and presses a button. A moment later, the ventilation system kicks in. "Better leave it running the whole time." She stays in the hall for safety, so I go over to her.

"Thanks. What's this about?"

"I tested two potential massage therapists, and they're both interested."

"Do you have a favorite?"

"They're both fantastic, so I'd suggest hiring both. One could come on weekday mornings until noon since he already has afternoon clients, and the other is free in the afternoons because he focuses on mornings. If we pay well, they're both willing to cover a few hours. That could work nicely."

"Did you let them work you over properly?" I tease.

London beams.

"Thoroughly—I feel reborn."

"Well, that's something. Once they start here, schedule me with one right away." I rub my neck, though it doesn't actually hurt. I just want to see her reaction.

"I could book you for this evening if you'd like. Even with another therapist."

"That would be too much trouble." I keep rubbing my neck. "I haven't boxed in a while either."

"Yeah..." London hesitates. I can see her fighting with herself, opening her mouth, closing it again. "I'll get you one as soon as possible." I wonder if she almost offered to do it herself.

"Thanks." She leaves, and I close the door, lost in thought. With some time left, I set up a quick meeting with my New York team. The time difference is only five hours—It's just 9:00 in the morning there and I want to answer some initial questions before my next appointment arrives.

The afternoon flies by. Between conversations, London comes back at one point with a fresh cup of coffee.

"I've managed to book you an appointment with a massage therapist. His practice is nearby. Full hour, six to seven."

That's what I get for asking.

"Perfect. Thanks a lot." Maybe it'll do me good after all.

"Can I ask you something else?" London looks nervous, almost excited.

"Go ahead." I wonder what's on her mind.

Chapter 15

London

He's the one who knows his father best. Well, except for Mr. Blackthorn himself of course, but I can't ask him right now.

"It's about the summer party on Friday—in two days at the country inn. Do you remember?" I ask. Alexander nods, sitting comfortably in his leather chair, watching me closely. "We'll work he until 1:00 PM, then everyone will be heading out. There are buses for most of the employees since three hundred and forty-four of them are coming. That is as long as no one cancels last-minute."

I'm lucky I'm a numbers whiz and can remember stuff like this effortlessly. "The festivities usually end by 8, but the last people leave around 9:00. It never goes too late—it's a summer party, after all."

"And how can I help with that?" he asks.

"Your father will give a speech, and I'm supposed to make sure he gets a proper farewell. I've planned several things, but I'm not entirely sure if he'll like them. I can still cancel or swap things out."

That's the upside of having a practically unlimited budget—you can buy almost anything.

"What have you planned?"

"Well, your father said it shouldn't be anything big, and if it is, then it should be something everyone enjoys. Everyone should have fun." I sigh. "Alcohol. Lots of alcohol. Private taxis."

"Yes, good. What else?"

"I managed to book Franky." The famous comedian has always made my boss laugh.

"Oh, great, he loves him"

"He'll do about thirty minutes of his new set. A band will also play your father's favorite songs. There'll be entertainers—men and women—getting people out on the dance floor. They'll set the mood."

"That all sounds great. Anything else?"

"Yes, I'm considering hiring Bonny Barns."

"The country singer?"

"Yes, your father's a big fan. She'd have to be flown in, though, and I need to decide now. She charges £300,000 plus flights, hotel, and extras."

"For...?"

"Three songs, maybe thirty minutes on stage. Then she leaves."

"Wow. I'd say book her privately some other time. He is a fan, but it would pull too much focus from the party."

"Yes, that's my concern too. The comedian's already a big name, but at least everyone will enjoy him."

"What about décor or food?"

"That stays as is. But I had a photo book printed with the best company pictures. A photographer's been here the last two days, shooting the offices, the parking lot, his office during a break..."

"That's really nice," Alex says.

"The photo book will be ready tomorrow; I can pick it up after work." I sigh softly. "If I'd had more time, I could've done more. Pulling this together in three days was exhausting. Then all the drama with you. God, I'm worn out." But happy. I smile. "You'll like the summer party."

"I'm looking forward to it."

"Okay, then I'll get back to work. I'm far from done. If you need me, just call." I hurry out of his office back to my desk. Time to focus. The faster I work, the better the odds I'll finish on time.

It works out reasonably well, at least. I stretch and glance at the clock. Only seventeen minutes overtime. Not bad.

I head back to my boss, who's with Alexander in his office. As always, I ask if they need anything else, but they say no. So, I leave—this time without eavesdropping.

Thursday is packed, so I eat lunch at my desk.

On Friday morning, the phones don't stop ringing. Just after 1:00, I finally shut down the computer and get ready for the party.

We've all earned this. Even though it doesn't officially start until 3:00, plenty of people will already be there enjoying themselves.

"Do you want to drive there together?" Alexander asks, appearing at my desk.

"Your father's being driven there in a limo. I'll leave my car here for now. You'll ride with us, right?"

"Perfect. Now we just need to get him out of his office. He really doesn't want to leave."

"I think I know why." I sigh and step closer. "He's probably saying goodbye to his office. He spent most of his working life there." But I wouldn't be the best PA if I hadn't prepared. "She's running a bit late, but she should be here any minute."

"She? Who?"

"Your mother." Alexander raises his eyebrows.

"My mother's coming?"

"Yes, she usually accompanies him to public events, and she especially wanted to come today."

"Do you two get along?"

"Yeah. Martha likes me." I grin, maybe bragging a little.

"Martha. My mother—*Martha Blackthorn*."

"Yes. Blonde bob, loves wearing white, bold gold earrings." I point down the hall, where she's already in view.

"Yoo-hoo!" calls Mrs. Blackthorn, beaming at me, which leaves Alexander speechless.

As she walks right toward me, he leans over and mutters, "My mother doesn't like anyone. Especially not young women."

"Then I must be the exception," I say cheerfully, opening my arms just before she pulls me into a tight hug and kisses me on both cheeks.

"You look absolutely delightful today, Miss Waverley," she gushes, placing her hands on my upper arms.

"That's rich coming from you. Not many women can pull off white, but you're radiant in it."

"A summery dress would certainly flatter you too. Are you changing?" she asks.

"Yes, I brought a dress, but I'll change there."

"Hair down? You absolutely must. You should have some fun today. After all, you've endured three hard years." She laughs, then turns to her son. "Well, aren't you going to say hello?"

"I didn't want to interrupt," Alexander replies, giving her a brief hug.

"What do you think? Doesn't your mother look chic?" She laughs and spins once. Her skin-tight white dress has a square neckline with wide sleeves. It falls to her knees and accentuates her firm ass. She doesn't look anywhere near fifty-two. The matching hat—also white, of course—pairs perfectly with her clutch and earrings.

"Of course."

"Aloof as always." She rolls her eyes, then turns back to me. "He's still in his office?" I nod. "You're a psychic."

I can't help smiling.

"In five minutes, he'll be out of there, or I'll drag him across the floor."

"If you need help…" I glance at Alex. "Your son's pretty strong."

"I can still handle him myself." She laughs and clicks away on her heels, leaving me alone with Alex again. He stares at me in surprise.

"How did you pull that off?"

"What do you mean?"

"That my mother is so friendly with you." He narrows his eyes skeptically. "Who are you?"

"I'm the mother-whisperer," I joke with a wink. Then I step closer, lowering my voice into a playfully threatening tone. "And you wanted to fire me? What do you think would've happened if I'd told your mother about that?"

"Looks like someone's got an ace up her sleeve?"

"Yeah, I'd say so!"

I reach for his tie and straighten it, tugging it a little tighter, which Alexander allows. "So be nice to me. You never know what a woman's next move will be."

"You seem to be full of secrets," he replies with a slight smile.

"A secret is what makes a woman a real woman."

"So, there's only one to figure out?"

"Countless. New ones every day. That's what makes talking to us exciting. We're completely different from you men." I adjust his suit, though there's hardly anything to fix. "You can be read like an open book."

"And what does mine say?" he asks, and his smile widens.

"Just because I know doesn't mean I have to tell you."

"But I am me. So, I know what's written there."

"But you don't know how I interpret it."

"Aren't you curious?" he asks.

"That's the real question."

"I'd have an answer for you."

"I know," I play along, even though I've long forgotten what the point of the game was.

"Are you interpreting it right?"

"I did before you even knew the answer," I tease, then step back. He studies me with an expression that's equal parts curious and fascinated. And oh yeah, I like that.

Martha appears in the hallway outside Mr. Blackthorn's office. A moment later Arthur follows. She slips her arm through his, and they approach us.

"Ready?" I ask Alexander, grabbing my bag.

"For mischief? Always."

"That too."

"What else?"

"It's a secret." We both laugh.

The four of us take the elevator down and as we exit the building, the first employees are already boarding the buses. Alexander walks me to my car because I want to grab my handbag from the trunk. He's kind enough to carry it while my boss and his wife settle into the limo.

The small shuttle buses and taxis are already pulling out of the lot. Alexander stands by the open limo door and offers me his hand so I can step in gracefully. The moment we touch, an inexplicably intense warmth rushes through me. I freeze for a moment and look at him, wondering what's happening to me.

Oh wow. This feels dangerously good.

Alexander's eyes lock on mine, and I realize I've been staring at him far too long. I force a quick smile and slide inside, hoping he didn't notice my odd reaction. He hands my bag to the driver, who places it in the trunk.

I sit across from Mrs. Blackthorn, and shortly after Alexander joins me, taking the seat at my side. The driver closes the door and circles to the front.

During the ride, Mrs. Blackthorn chats to her husband. She gushes about how he finally has more time for her, and how they can enjoy retirement together. But I can clearly see his mind is still tethered to the company. It'll take time before he can fully embrace being just a husband emotionally—and at most, a consultant. For now, at least, he humors her, while Alexander sits silently, gazing out the window.

We're among the first to reach the Country Inn. Here, outside of London, I pause a moment, taking in the peace and quiet, before the driver opens the door. Alexander steps out first, then his father. I let Mrs. Blackthorn go ahead, then climb out last. Once again, Alexander offers me his hand. I try not to let his warm touch unravel me, and head with him to the trunk, where the driver retrieves my bag. I take it.

"I'm curious what dress you brought," Alexander says.

"A simple one," I admit sheepishly, then gesture toward the courtyard. "So, how do you like it?"

Alexander studies the large three-story building, wrapped in greenery. Trees, shrubs, flower beds—it all feels inviting. And the weather couldn't be more perfect.

We leave the paved path in the secluded parking lot and head toward the entrance. The ground changes to cobblestones, though they're laid so evenly you could walk on them in high heels without worry.

"Makes a good impression," he says.

"You probably thought we'd be celebrating in a luxury hotel, didn't you?" I ask.

"Honestly, yeah. But I'm curious to see what the afternoon brings."

We reach the reception area just outside the entrance. Standing tables draped in white tablecloths are set up, with chilled drinks, tea, and coffee already being served generously to the first guests.

"We've booked the entire inn. All the rooms are open if anyone wants to freshen up or change. You just grab a key and return it afterward."

"Then I'll see you soon?"

"I won't be long," I promise, stepping inside.

I like this rustic vibe. Everything's heavy with wood, giving it a cozy, country look. The white-plastered walls are dotted with dried plants as decoration. Somehow—even that fits right in.

I take one of the room keys, seize the chance to freshen up, and change into the outfit I brought along. But while I'm turning back and forth in front of the mirror, I have the sudden urge to call my best friend.

"Hey, do you have a minute?" I start chattering as I sit on the bed, makeup brush in hand. Before Vanessa can even answer, I keep rambling: "Something happened, and I absolutely have to talk about it!"

"Well, go ahead," she says with a quiet laugh. Sometimes I just can't help myself—I talk like a waterfall. Terrible.

"Alex touched my hand." I draw the words out like I'd just met the king and been granted a handshake.

"Okay?" She sounds puzzled. "I need context, my dear," she says, laughing as I hear her walking through her apartment. A bottle opens with a *pop* and fizz. Hopefully it's just sparkling water and not champagne. She's been drinking a bit too much lately.

"We were driven from the office in the limo to the inn I already told you about, right?"

"I remember," she says.

"Well, when we got in, he was so sweet and offered me his hand to help me. And I took it." Silence.

"Okay… and then?"

"We touched. He held my hand."

"Uh, yeah, I got that. But what am I supposed to say? I need more context, London… was it awkward, or… wait. Wait!"

"Yes!" Finally, she gets it.

"Oh my God!"

"Yes! Exactly! Oh my God times ten!"

"Holy crap!"

"You can say that again!"

"Holy cow patties on toast, fuck, that's… are you sure?"

"Cow patties? What?"

"Fits with a country inn, doesn't it?" she teases.

"There aren't any cows here. There are apple trees. They've gone completely overboard with the apple theme. Apples everywhere. Pictures on the walls: apples. Wallpaper: apples. The soap? Apple-shaped and apple-scented. The headboard? Carved with…"

"Apples?"

"Branches with apples on them." Silence again.

"Forget the apples," Vanessa sighs. "So, you touched him and suddenly it went *ka-ching*?" She mimics a shrill bell.

"Kind of. It felt good. I mean, *really* good..."

"And you don't like that?"

"He's my boss."

"Well, he's good-looking. And a real gentleman."

"He. Is. My. Boss."

"Polite and friendly, too."

"Nessa. He is my BOSS."

"Really? He's your boss? Gee, I had no idea. You never told me that," she shoots back sarcastically, then sighs. "It's wonderful you got a good vibe from him. Maybe it doesn't mean anything. After all, you've been single forever."

"Yeah..." Like cobwebs between my legs and crickets chirping with an echo when I spread them.

"Well, if I've learned anything from Dominic, it's this: Life's short and guys can always screw you over. So, enjoy it. Sleep with him. Have fun. Keep it a secret. Just enjoy yourself."

"Have you been drinking again?"

"No."

"Liquor-filled chocolates?"

"Maybe."

"Oh, Nessa..."

"And I have a date tonight. A sex date. Met him on an app. We're having dinner, then I'm staying at his place all night. And then I'll never call him again!" Sounds like a plan.

"Is this revenge on all men everywhere?"

"No, I just want to enjoy single life without feelings." She sighs. "I don't want to sit here crying, drinking, overeating, and being miserable. That doesn't change what happened. So, it doesn't matter if I go on a date today or three months from now. I mean, he didn't die or anything. He was just an ass, and I won't let him ruin my life."

"If you were sober right now, I might actually believe you, my dear..." She's never drunk this much before. I just hope this guy treats her well tonight—and that she slows down with the drinking. "Will you send me the hotel address and his details?"

"Of course." That's our unspoken rule, but with her a little buzzed, I'd better say it outright, so she doesn't forget. These days, women have to be extra careful. Too many creeps walk around free who should be locked up. And you can't always tell right away when a guy's off.

"When are you meeting him?" I ask.

"He's picking me up at seven. We're going to the Blue Seastar—right downtown. Fancy restaurant. So either he's got money, or he's just planning to stick me with the bill," she laughs. "If he's nice, I'll go home with him. He offered to come to my place, but honestly, it's a mess right now."

"I'll come over this weekend and help you clean." I owe her that much. After all, I helped cause the mess.

"Oh, I can handle it. But if you want to come over for a movie night, you're more than welcome."

"Before that, I need to visit Alex. He's still looking for a housekeeper. I told him I knew someone, but... I meant me."

"What? Why would you want to clean for him?"

"Because it gives me a chance to get to know him better—and for him to know me. It's only temporary, until he finds someone permanent. Probably just a weekend or two."

"Or are you doing it for the money? Haven't you saved enough already?"

"I have. But this is a convenient opportunity. If I'm at his place, and we get along—maybe even become friends, he'll be more likely to keep me on. You see what I mean?"

"Yeah, I get it. Fine. But I'll clean my place alone, and you can come over afterward, okay?"

"We could cook something together?" I suggest.

"Or order pizza," she counters immediately.

"Pizza sounds good too." I pause, then return to what she suggested. "I'll keep my hands off him. It feels good to talk about this with you. At least you get me," I sigh softly.

"That's what best friends are for," she says warmly. Then she cackles and demands, "Now go throw yourself at him! And tell me everything afterward."

"You're impossible." I laugh, then say goodbye.

Afterward, I slip into my sandals with delicate ankle straps and smooth my dress—a white one with bold blue flowers, cinched with a gold belt. My hair falls loose, my jewelry subtle.

Yes, girl. You look great.

But when I look into the mirror I can't help but wonder: Will Alexander like what he sees?

I roll my eyes at myself. Love should stay far, far away from me. I don't have time for that. Especially not with him. Nope. Never him. Ever.

Chapter 16

Alexander

I follow my parents toward the garden. A huge lake spreads, dotted with ducks and swans. Countless apple trees line the paths, a small stage draped in white fabric stands ready for the band, and groups of tables with benches, chairs, and other sitting areas. The adjacent hall is open, and the large event room in the main building is already packed. Buffets are set up in several spots, while grill masters stoke their fires. There's something for everyone—barbecue, vegan food, salads, snacks... And also, ice cream, whole cakes, layered cakes, and muffins.

I grab a bowl of watermelon and honeydew melon and scan the crowd. Most employees have gathered in small groups, enjoying themselves. The band takes the stage and starts playing a moment later and it's not too loud, so conversations can continue easily.

"Well, tell me honestly, my dear son—how do you like her?" my mother asks, holding a champagne flute filled with orange juice.

"Her?" I suspect she's referring to London, but I'd rather avoid this conversation. The way she's smiling tells me exactly where this is going.

"You know who I mean. London. She's smart, dedicated, loyal, and pretty. You'd have the most adorable children if you got married."

Here we go.

My father is absolutely delighted and feels validated. "That's exactly what I told him!" Of course—the one time they agree, it has to be about this.

A server comes along, offering alcohol, and I take a glass gladly. God knows I need some champagne right now.

"You're planning to get drunk?" my mother whispers.

"Every time you try to set me up with London, I'm drinking a glass of champagne. So, it's up to you whether I get drunk today or not." I raise my glass, take a good sip, and put the empty flute back on the tray.

"I was just saying you'd make a gorgeous couple, and—" she starts to backpedal.

I don't even let the server leave before I snag another glass.

"Alex, please," she protests, indignantly.

I don't drink it right away.

"She's going to be my PA. I expect professionalism. From both sides." That should make my position clear.

My mother, however, snatches the glass from my hand and puts it back on the tray before shooing the server away. "You won't find anyone better. I've spent three years vetting her thoroughly."

"You did what?" I ask, irritated.

"I know everything. Who her friends are, where her parents and brothers work, whether she has debts, her criminal record... I'm telling tell you: this woman is perfect."

I swear she won't stop until London is carrying my child.

"Not in this lifetime, Mother. But you're still young, you could have another son if you're so desperate to dictate someone's life. At least until he hits puberty."

I chuckle, amused while she gives me a death glare. That ice-cold smile with the rigid eyes is something any son should fear.

"Well, your mother isn't that young anymore," my father says lightly, immediately receiving the full force of her glare. "That's not what I meant, honey," he says with a laugh.

Time for me to make an escape and talk to other people. But as I turn, ready to disappear, London walks toward us.

That white dress with its bold blue flowers is stunning, cinched with a gold belt that matches her sandals and jewelry. Her hair falls loose around her shoulders.

Until now, I'd only seen her in athletic wear. Now, in a summer dress...

"Oh, look who's stopping dead at the sight of London?" my mother teases as she moves beside me. "I'm already planning your wedding. The only question is—where should it be? Paris would be lovely, don't you think?"

It's hard to tear my gaze from London to glare at my grinning mother instead.

"I'm not a fan of France," I say, then give London a brief nod of greeting. She glances at me a little embarrassed, brushing her hair back.

"You look fantastic," my mother says, immediately pulling her over, while my father settles in next to us with some snacks.

"Thank you," London answers, then looks shyly at me again.

I just nod in silence. What else can I say? She looks fantastic. Her figure is shown off perfectly, and with her hair down she looks so much more feminine. Did she change her makeup? Her lips look like a different color. My gaze lingers there for a moment before I force myself to look away.

Not good. I should definitely not be thinking about her—whether it's in a summer dress or workout clothes.

Absolutely not.

The afternoon slips by quickly—at least for me. Employees keep coming up to welcome me back, asking the same questions over and over, and I give them the same polite answers. I remain friendly, respectful, professional—even though by the hundredth time I really don't want to hear another "So how was New York?" Maybe I should've just sent a company-wide email beforehand.

I keep catching glimpses of London, animatedly chatting with the department heads. A few female employees are watching her with daggers in their eyes, while my mother keeps throwing me knowing glances.

"Don't think I haven't noticed how you keep watching her," she murmurs as she passes by. Determined to put an end to this, I follow her.

"I observe everyone. Especially her. I want to know how well London gets along with the others. Seems like she's not too popular with the women here?"

We stop at the buffet, filling our plates. I go heavy on the protein-rich foods, though I allow myself some fruit too today.

"Women in high positions are always targets for envy. And she's attractive—and didn't sleep her way to the top. But of course, there are always rumors. Those women are itching to gossip, hoping for a juicy scandal." My mother smiles knowingly. "And now that my handsome son is in charge, they're probably waiting to see when her belly starts to grow."

I sigh quietly and just walk away, which seems to amuse her. At least she's enjoying herself. For me, this whole thing is edging toward boring.

So, I slip away. Just for a moment. The comedian has taken the stage, and I can finally breathe. Everyone's already seen me and shaken my hand, so who's going to notice if I disappear for a bit?

With a plate piled high and a glass of apple juice, I head inside. The building is nearly empty, except for a few employees restocking the buffet. At reception, I grab one of the keys and climb the stairs. No one around. The quiet feels like heaven compared to the noise outside. If I lie down for a while, I'll have more energy later.

Upstairs, I unlock room 100. But behind me, I hear a sound. I turn—and there she is. London. She's just coming out of room 99, directly across from mine.

"Most people take the lower numbers, so they don't have to walk up the stairs. There's no elevator here," she says awkwardly, cheeks flushed.

"That's why I came up here. Just wanted to rest a bit and escape the noise," I answer. Damn, she looks really good when she's shy like that. She tucks a strand of hair behind her ear.

No, don't—it looked better before.

One hand rests on her stomach. Is she okay?

"Are you alright?"

"I think I just had a little too much to drink," she admits.

Ah. So, the flushed cheeks aren't because of me, but the alcohol.

"There was hardly any alcohol in the champagne I had earlier," I probe.

"I might just be on good terms with the supplier. I've been in touch with them for three years…" She grins. "The good stuff is somewhere else."

"I see." I raise my brows, surprised.

"I don't usually drink much. Just once in a while. I was just telling my best friend today she should stop—but here I am." She sighs, fumbling with her key ring while trying to close the door.

"Yeah, you've definitely had a bit too much," I comment.

"It's fine. I'll just grab a coffee or two and sit somewhere."

"Or you could lie down, and I'll drive you home," I offer.

"But you've been drinking too," she points out.

"Just one glass of champagne. Barely any alcohol in it. I couldn't even taste it."

"But then you'll miss the party," she argues.

"It's almost over anyway."

"People will gossip if they don't see us anymore…" And she's not wrong. "I'll mingle a little longer. Once I'm sober, I'll drive home." At least she's steady on her feet.

"You're not driving anywhere tonight. It's obvious you've had too much." I step closer. "Didn't you say this ends by 9 at the latest? I'll call a driver to take us both home. Then I can enjoy a few more drinks. But for you, the night's over."

"Is that an order?" she asks, her tone carrying something that makes me believe she's flirting with me.

"Exactly. This is a company event—you follow your boss's instructions."

"But you're not my boss until Monday."

I give her a sharp look.

"Aye, aye, Captain."

"Good. I'll come get you later. Don't forget your bag."

"I'll come back for it." London nods sweetly, then heads down the hallway. She's still walking straight. Good.

I take a deep breath and step into my room, closing the door. Dropping onto the bed, I stare at the ceiling.

Should I have pushed her to stay? We could've talked. But no—I can't let myself get caught up in this. It's just a crazy thought, nothing more. Yes, she's hot, and yes, the temptation to sleep with her is real. But it would destroy our working relationship—and brutally so.

Chapter 17

London

That was a close call.

I hadn't actually had much to drink, but my cheeks burned so hot that I couldn't think of another excuse. I just didn't want him to believe I was blushing because of him—even though that's exactly what was happening.

At the stairs, I pause to catch my breath. My things can stay upstairs for now; I'll grab them before heading home for the weekend. I should rejoin the crowd anyway—and maybe grab a few more snacks. I'm still quite hungry.

It's a good hour later when I see Alexander again as I stroll near the lake. The fresh air feels good, and I let myself have a drink or two—just enough to relax but still stay in control.

I want to try something, and for that, I'll need a little courage from the champagne.

Gradually, people start heading home. It really was a beautiful summer party—speeches, music, , entertaining performances, good food, and wonderful weather. The day couldn't have gone any better. By just before 9, only a handful of people are left, saying their goodbyes one by one, until finally just the top executives remain.

Alexander comes over to his parents, while I'm standing next to them.

"Oh, how sweet of our son," Mrs. Blackthorn chirps happily when I tell her Alexander has offered to drive me home.

"Do you want to take the limo?" Mr. Blackthorn asks as Alexander joins me.

"I'll drive myself," Alexander replies. "I only had a few sips of champagne hours ago." He looks at me and can't stop himself from smiling. "But you'll be sitting properly in the passenger seat."

"And how am I supposed to get my car back?" I ask. I can't exactly show up to work on Monday without it.

"I'll pick you up Monday and drive you in," he offers.

"But I need my car over the weekend," I counter.

"Then I'll have it brought to you. That's what the staff is for. Just give me your spare key, and they'll park it right at your door."

That sounds much better.

"Well, you two will figure it out," Mrs. Blackthorn says, tugging at her husband's sleeve. "Come on, let's head home too."

"I'll stop by sometime this week, Miss Waverley—but only briefly," my soon-to-be former boss says.

"Yes, yes. Very rarely. I'll make sure of that."

His wife doesn't seem thrilled by the idea. She hugs me quickly, then her son, while my boss simply shakes both our hands.

"Well, you two enjoy your evening." Then she pulls her husband away, leaving Alexander and me alone at the venue while the staff starts clearing up.

"Can you grab your things or should I?" he asks.

"Hmm, I'm feeling a little dizzy," I lie. In truth, I'd had some champagne but could've driven myself just fine.

Still, my little shit-test wouldn't work otherwise.

"Alright. Then wait for me out front, and I'll grab your things from Room 99."

Alexander starts walking, and I trail behind with deliberately unsteady steps. He places a steadying hand on my back. "Are you okay?"

"Yes, no problem," I fib again. Sweet—he's worried. First point for him.

He escorts me to the reception area, where I sink onto a bench outside. It gives me a moment to collect myself before Alexander returns with my bag.

"All set." He offers his hand, and I'm only too happy to take his arm as we walk to the parking lot. Two employees are waiting with two limos. One is for us; they'll return with the other.

Alexander opens the passenger door for me, then has a quick word with the employees. He hands them my car key—the spare is at my apartment. Alexander comes over to me and asks: "What's your address?"

I give it to him so he can give further instructions to the two employees before he stows my bag in the back seat before climbing in beside me.

Meanwhile, his parents are being escorted to their own car by another driver.

"Seat belt on?" he asks with a raised brow. No, not yet. "How much did you drink?"

"Just a little," I mumble, feigning to be much more tired than I actually am. Alexander leans over to me - and boom, I'm wide awake. I stare at him with wide-open eyes, but thankfully he doesn't notice. He pulls the seat belt across me, buckles it, and says, "If you want to sleep, go ahead. We'll be on the road at least ninety minutes."

"Are you going through the city?"

"No, around it. At this hour, traffic in London would take us more than two hours."

"That's a big detour for you, isn't it?"

"It's only about thirty minutes from your place to mine. Not a big deal," he assures me, fastening his own belt.

"Thanks for doing this," I say, watching him start the car.

"I'm already the best boss in the world, aren't I?" he teases with a smile that makes me drift into a little daydream.

"Top ten," I joke, my gaze sliding down his body. His hands especially catch my eye—strong, masculine. The watch on his wrist looks ridiculously good on him. Why is it that men with watches are so damn hot? Just before pulling out, he rolls his sleeves up a bit, revealing his toned forearms. Although I've seen him train shirtless before with his whole torso bare, somehow this—just the two of us alone in the car—feels completely different. Heat curls through me as I stare. Then I glance up and startle—he's looking right at me, and I'm pretty sure he caught me staring.

"Want to take a picture?" he asks audaciously.

"You're impossible…" I deflect, blush, and turn to the window. "Shame it's still so bright out. The sun's setting, but it won't be fully dark for at least another hour."

"Do you prefer driving at night?" he asks as he steers us onto the road. The gentle rocking of the car calms me, but it also makes me more aware of the alcohol in my system. I glance at him, wondering if he has any idea how attractive I find him.

"No, it's about the stars."

"Because London is too bright, you mean?"

"Yeah… Out here, with all the fields and forests, there's no big city lights so the sky gets dark enough to see them. We get so used to not looking for stars anymore, even though we know they're always there. And when you finally see them, it's just… beautiful. The universe is infinite and simply… beautiful."

I probably sound ridiculous.

"I know what you mean. We shouldn't just accept the brightness of the cities—we should notice nature more."

"Yes…" I sigh. Amn, I can't help yawning. This time I don't even have to fake it; drowsiness is settling in for real.

"You could stretch out on the back seat," he offers. The car's as luxurious inside as it looks from the outside—the seats are wide and soft. It's tempting. But then I wouldn't be able to watch him anymore.

"I'm fine. I don't want to leave you driving alone." Another yawn.

"Just don't make me catch your yawns," he laughs, merging onto the main road.

"Can I ask you something?"

"Of course."

"I only heard this in passing today, but you must have answered it a hundred times: Why did you really go to New York back then?"

Alexander laughs. "Yeah, almost everyone wanted to know that. I always said I found the city fascinating and wanted to experience it, but the truth is I wanted to prove myself. In London, everyone who's someone knows who I am. I wanted to succeed without my father's help. And I did. It felt really good. But of course, I couldn't say that to the staff."

I catch his words while being gently rocked back and forth.

"Do you miss New York?" I ask, stifling another yawn.

"Oh yes. Very much." His expression softens. "But I'm the only son. It's my responsibility to take over the company. That's my burden—and my duty. Still, New York is something special and I miss it a lot. Life there is different. People are more relaxed, more open-minded. I had good friends there who didn't know who I was. That was a gift—it helped me figure out who was genuinely with me."

The next thing I know, his warm hand touches mine, and the car isn't moving.

"Huh?"

"Hey, sleepyhead. We're here."

I blink at him, startled. Alexander unbuckles his seatbelt while I stare through the windshield in confusion, because all I see is: nothing. It's pitch black. We're definitely not at my place—there are no streetlights or brightly lit windows.

"I didn't mean to fall asleep," I mumble, yawning again as I unbuckle my belt.

"I must've been boring you," he teases. "But I think this is the perfect spot."

"Perfect spot?"

"Yeah." He steps out of the car, while I sit there, confused. The interior light illuminates him briefly.

I unbuckle my seatbelt and open my door. A cool breeze slips under my dress and wakes me up instantly. During the day, with the sun still out, it was wonderfully warm, but now this late in the evening, it cooled down quickly. The grass beneath my feet confirms we're in the middle of nowhere.

"Please tell me my eyes are the problem and you're not planning to bury me in the woods," I say. Slowly, my eyes are adjusting to the darkness. There are headlights flickering in the distance. Alexander comes around to my side.

"I hadn't planned on it," he says, placing a steadying hand at the small of my back and nudging me away from the open door so he can close it. "Cold?"

"No, it's actually quite pleasant," I mumble. "It especially helps to clear my head."

Alone with him in the dark, at least he can't see how red my cheeks are—but I can definitely feel the heat in them.

"Sit," he says gently, guiding me to the hood. We lean against it together. Slowly I can make out more, which is also due to the brilliantly bright full moon that is clearly visible in the sky. Wait. What am I thinking? In amazement, I stare at the sky, which is so clear and beautiful above us that I can hardly believe it.

"Look!" I tug at his sleeve, pointing upward. "It's so bright! And the stars too!"

Only then do I realize where we are. Somewhere in the middle of nowhere—far enough from any city that would light-pollute the night sky. Above us, thousands, no, millions… actually, billions of stars glitter. My mouth falls open as I marvel at the Milky Way and the constellations shine sharp and clear. Venus. The North Star. All visible.

Alexander lies back on the hood, turning a small USB stick in his fingers before slipping it into his pocket. He really has that thing with him all the time, like some kind of talisman. Then he folds his hands behind his head and stares upward, surely enjoying the view as much as I do.

"This is gorgeous," I whisper enthusiastically, lying down beside him. The hood radiates warmth beneath me, while the night is cool and fresh. It's a perfect combination, with a priceless, magnificent view.

I sense Alexander watching me before he finally says, "True."

I turn my face toward him and smile. "This is the most beautiful thing anyone's ever done for me."

"Really?"

"Yes. No diamond ring in the world, no luxury car or anything else could top this."

"Sounds like you're hinting for a lavish Christmas gift from your boss," he teases with a wide smile.

"As long as you show me the stars, my world's perfect." I turn my gaze back to the night sky. My heart has calmed in his presence, and I relax, infinitely comfortable. I have to admit: that's another point for him. "Do you do this for all your employees?"

"Yes, I'll be very busy for the next few months," he deadpans, and we both burst out laughing.

"And here I thought I was something special," I say nervously, glancing at him.

Alexander just smiles.

"Do you really *think* that—or do you *know* it?" he finally asks.

"I know I'm something special, yes." My eyes linger on his lips. My pulse kicks up. "May I be honest with you?" Now or never. He drove me here, under this sky, and this glowing moon. There won't be a better moment.

"Of course. As long as it has nothing to do with the church."

"No." That again. I can't help but laugh softly and lean a little closer. "Well, maybe just a tiny bit—since that's where we first met."

I brace myself on one arm and lean over him. His lips curve into a gentle smile as he watches me. His lips form a gentle smile and then—my courage deserts me.

He's my boss, damn it. I can't. I flop back down, eyes darting up at the stars instead. That's safer. Safer than imagining what his kiss might feel like.

"Why didn't you do it?" he asks quietly, propping himself up now. The question knocks the air out of me and I wonder if he knows I wanted to kiss him.

"What do you mean?" I try to deflect.

"Then I'll do it."

Before I can react, Alexander leans closer, smiling as his hand cups my cheek and carefully approaches my lips. I take one last deep breath, while I lie there stiff as a board, holding my breath and closing my eyes, until our lips touch. A surge of tingling shoots through me - it's much more intense and beautiful than I could have ever dreamed. Alexander's warm lips lock against mine, while he simultaneously caresses my cheek with his hand. Whether it's the alcohol or his skills, I'm not quite sure, but I don't want to think about it anymore because it feels fantastic.

Oh, if only time would stop!

I never want to do anything else but lie here and be kissed. In this moment, I don't care about anything. Absolutely anything. Like the fact that he's my boss. I'll worry about that later. Away with the concerns. Bring on the hot butterflies in my stomach and pure desire.

"I've wanted to do that the whole time," he murmurs against my lips, smiling.

I just stare at him in disbelief.

The whole time? So, I wasn't imagining it? The looks, the subtle tension, even that scene of him undressing in front of me... all real.

"And now you just *stop*?" I ask dumbfounded. My hands slide up to his cheeks and I tug him back down to me. Greedy kisses on a car hood under London's magnificent starry sky - excuse me? Could it get any more romantic? I don't think so.

I loop my arms around his neck, fingers threading into his hair, one leg shifting so he can lie over me more easily. But what does he do? Nothing.

"How much have you actually had to drink, hmm?" he whispers against my lips.

"Just a tiny bit. Promise," I lie.

"What if you don't remember this tomorrow?"

"I'm perfectly lucid."

"No, you're not. I can still taste the alcohol." He presses a tender kiss to my forehead. "But I'm glad for it. It gave you enough courage to kiss me. Made you loosen up a bit."

"You too," I murmur, stroking his face.

"I only had a few sips. You, apparently, had a whole bottle."

"It was a very small one. Honestly."

"Maybe in the world of giants," he teases, then gets up and offers me his hand. "Come on. It's not far to your place."

"Are you inviting yourself over?" I ask boldly, slipping my hand into his.

"I'm just the driver, making sure the precious cargo gets safely to bed."

To bed? That makes me giggle.

"You're really cute when you've been drinking," he adds, "but I like you better sober."

I trail behind him, still holding his hand. When he opens the passenger door, I press it shut again with my palm.

"I think I want to lie down in the back seat," I say, feigning tipsiness a little more. Another test for you, *Mister Irresistible*.

"That's a really good idea." He opens the back door. But as I go to climb in, I cling to him, tugging at his shirt.

"Have you ever had sex under the stars? Be honest."

"Not yet," he replies with a wicked smirk. "But it's not going to happen tonight either."

"You don't *want* to?" I ask him with a hungry look.

"If you were sober, then yes. But not like this." He chuckles softly and helps me into the car. Another point for him—but I'm still left wanting. Though... the night's not over yet.

I lie down on the back seat, and he closes the door and gets back in the front. The gentle movements of the car feel wonderful, and unfortunately, the bit of alcohol in my blood makes me fall asleep again.

When I wake again, I'm in his arms.

"What?" I mumble, clinging to him in surprise. He's taken me out of the car, and I didn't notice at all. Since when do I sleep so deeply?

"Well, someone's awake again," he says with a grin. I blink and look around. Yes—this is my building's parking lot.

"Yeah." Lying in his arms, one arm tucked beneath my knees and the other supporting my back, sends tingles racing through me. I'm close to him again—but now, under the bright artificial glow of the streetlamps, I can see him so much more clearly. "You can put me down." I should still be able to walk. "I could make you some coffee to keep you awake for the drive back," I offer as he gently sets me down.

"I won't say no to coffee. But only if you also show me your stamp collection," he demands.

"I actually have one," I reply with feigned surprise, even though of course I don't. Alex looks genuinely astonished as he grabs my bag and locks the car.

"Well then..."

I clutch my handbag, fish out the key, and thank heavens there's an elevator in this building. We walk to it and ride up in silence, stealing only a few brief glances at each other.

I unlock my apartment door smoothly. If he thinks I'm not tipsy anymore, maybe he'll stay. Nessa did say I should have fun. Once doesn't count. Wait—did she really say that? I can't remember, but it *sounds* like something she'd say. Or maybe it was just me.

"How lucky I cleaned yesterday," I mutter as I let him in and switch on the light. Oof. That's blinding.

"Where should I put the bag?" he asks. I take it from him.

"Make yourself at home. Bathroom's across from the bedroom, and this is the living room." I point in each direction. "I'll take this to my bedroom first." Alex nods, and I slip away quickly.

I hurry past the living room and bathroom into my bedroom, where I scoop up the pairs of underwear I'd tossed beside the bed instead of into the laundry basket. The bag lands neatly at the foot of the bed. A quick spray of room fragrance—and I head back out.

Alexander is standing in the kitchen, fiddling with the coffee maker. Okay. He really *does* want that drink.

"Would you like one too?" he asks, glancing over at me.

"You're my guest. Sit down."

More caffeine now? That'll keep me awake all night. But maybe that's not such a bad thing—depending on whether he plans to stay.

Instead of sitting, he leans casually against the counter, eyes locked on me. The way he watches only makes me more nervous. My hand slips, and I end up spilling a little coffee.

Chapter 18

Alexander

This little liar. Typical woman with her little *shitty* tests. I wonder if I've passed them all. I would've loved to take her right there on the hood of the car—or in the backseat at the very least. Instead, I'm standing here watching her shaky hands as she tries to measure coffee grounds into the machine.

It's cute that she's pretending to be tipsy, but she's not fooling me. Still, I'll play along—it's entertaining either way.

"You've got a nice place," I say, looking around more closely. She has plenty of houseplants, and the space is clean, organized, and functional. But there are also lots of personal touches—like the large board on the wall opposite the counter, covered with photos of her and her best friend. "I don't see any pictures of your brothers or parents," I remark.

"Hmm, yeah..." she mumbles, adding water to the machine before switching it on and opening the fridge. "I could make us something to eat. Or I've got chips, if you're in the mood?" She's trying to change the subject.

"You don't get along with them?" I press. Her rigid gaze gives her away. Sure, she's had a few drinks, but not nearly enough to not know what she's doing.

"It's complicated," she admits, pulling out a salad in a red bowl. She stirs it with two large spoons. "Chicken, cucumbers, lettuce, corn, and kidney beans. Very high in protein," she explains.

"Except for the corn," I point out. Then I add, "But I'd love some."

"Dressing? I have light honey-mustard, or homemade yogurt."

"Yogurt."

She's dodging my question again. "Do you find it uncomfortable to talk about your family?"

"Is it that obvious?" she asks nervously, though she's still smiling. Looks like I hit a nerve. London takes two smaller bowls and fills them generously. She hands me one with a fork.

"Must've been hard growing up with three older brothers," I say.

"Yeah, true." She gestures toward the couch and heads there. I follow, the coffee brewing behind us. We sit down, only about twenty inches apart. "Vanessa says I sometimes act like a guy, because I always had to hold my own when I was younger. There wasn't much time to be a girl."

"Strict father?"

"Oh yeah." She raises her brows and widens her eyes. Must've been bad.

"No mother to intervene?"

"I love my parents and brothers, really. But I'm glad I don't have to be around them all the time. My father would have loved a fourth son, and that's how he raised me. He hated when I wore dresses. When puberty hit and I wanted makeup, he was devastated. When my brothers wrestled with me—even if I was crying or hurt—he cheered them on and told me to fight back. But how could I, when they were so much stronger? I was always covered in bruises. They didn't know their own strength. It was like locking a Pomeranian in a room with three pit bulls."

"Did they hurt you on purpose?" I ask, shocked.

"No. We were kids, and they were boys. Later, when we were older, we argued a lot. One would hold me down while another took something from me—even if it was just dessert. They were always a unit. Still are today. It's like I never really belonged. Sometimes..." She pauses, poking at her salad. "Sometimes I think I was adopted. My parents treat them so differently—much more love, more affection. They always ask how my brothers are doing, what they're up to. Everything revolves around them. Family parties and events are planned around their schedules, never mine. But I've gotten used to it." She smiles bravely. "You can't choose your family. Over the years, I've built my own. My best friend Vanessa—Nessa—is like the sister I never had. I wish we'd met sooner. That would've been amazing."

"When did you meet?"

"Online." She laughs sweetly, making me smile instantly. I love that look on her. "When I moved in here, I was searching for nice second-hand things to decorate. By chance, I found her ad—she was selling plant cuttings. I thought: Hey, cool idea. So, I messaged her. We chatted for hours until she suggested moving to the phone. We hit it off right away. Then she came over." London points to her plants. "That was over three years ago. Every one of these pretty babies started tiny. Haven't lost a single one." She looks proud. "Just like our friendship. She hasn't always had it easy either. I think that's why we click."

I take a bite of salad, then she starts eating too. It feels good, sitting here with her. But I also want to be honest. "I know you're not drunk."

London stares at me, shocked.

"Did I pass your little tests? If so, great—I'll stay. But if you're going to keep pretending, I'll leave after coffee." She's speechless and doesn't even swallow her salad. "You're way too easy to read," I laugh, eating more while she sits there, face red, unable to respond. Finally, she swallows and pokes at her salad, as if she might find the answer she so desperately needs hidden among the leaves.

She sneaks a glance at me, then takes a breath. "I wanted to know if you'd take advantage."

"I wouldn't." I set down my bowl, take hers too, and place them both on the table. With my thumb, I wipe dressing from her lips, then lick it clean. "I want you to enjoy every second when we sleep together. I want you to remember it."

Her cheeks flush again, making me grin. Her face is like a mirror for her emotions.

"Do you sleep with all your PAs?" she asks.

"Only the ones who can keep up with me in sports."

I manage to make her laugh.

"What kind of women are those?"

"Strong, independent women with an indomitable will." I kiss her cheek and lean in. A sweet sigh escapes her warm mouth, which I kiss shortly after. Mm. She's delicious.

"Won't this affect our work relationship?" she asks, even as I'm already thinking about carrying her to bed.

"Only positively."

I want more...

"Do you think I'm doing this just because..." I know where she's headed, so I silence her with another kiss. I don't want to hear anything about ambition or sleeping her way up. I just want her. Naked under me. To explore her body with my tongue and hear how eagerly she moans when I fuck her in the wildest positions. "It's just that I... will this be a one-time thing?"

"If that's what you want," I answer simply.

"You're my boss," she reminds me.

"Starting Monday. Right now, you don't have one. Not for three more days."

I kiss her neck, tasting her soft skin.

Oh yeah, not bad at all. I really like this.

Her little whimpers drive me wild. Her voice alone turns me on. I slip a hand onto her thigh immediately. I've been imagining this whole time—now it's finally happening.

"So this is legitimate. You won't treat me differently when we start working together on Monday?"

"Promise." My hand slides under her dress just as the coffee maker beeps. Who wants coffee when I could be slipping this gorgeous woman's panties off?

"And you're not just saying that to get me into bed?" she asks, pressing her hands lightly against my chest to half-heartedly push me back a few inches. Her gaze is serious, full of concern.

"I'm a gentleman. No one will know and it won't affect our working relationship. If you mess up, I'll fire you. If you're good, you'll stay on."

"Okay." She seems satisfied.

So, can I continue?

Perfect.

I pull her onto my lap to get better access to explore and touch everything. London weighs nothing compared to the weights I lift. She straddles me, hands on my chest again, while mine roam her back.

She feels amazing.

It's like unwrapping a gift. There's even a bow. How fitting. I slide both hands under her dress, caressing her thighs until I find her firm ass. I pull her closer, and she lets out another surprised but eager sigh. She presses against my chest, caresses my cheeks, and kisses me exploratively. It feels like she hasn't been touched in far too long. Or is she always this responsive?

Her gasps and eager panting turn me on incredibly. My hardness strains against my boxers and pants. I want to see her come. I want to hear what this gorgeous woman sounds like when she orgasms

And I already know: this won't be just a one-time thing.

Chapter 19

London

I can't remember the last time I was this aroused. My heart is pounding, my pulse is so loud I swear he must hear it. It's these small, gentle touches of his large, warm, and strong hands exploring my body that completely undo me. He's taking his time. A lot of time. Alexander is a true connoisseur, savoring every tiny detail of this one-time thing.

It is just a one-time thing, right? Afterward we'll go back to boss and assistant. No office affair. Nothing. Right? I don't want to sleep my way to the top, and I definitely don't want to make him fall in love with me just so I can keep my job. I simply want him. He's hot. Damn hot. And I never thought he'd actually be interested in me.

But what if he *is* taking advantage? What if he thinks I'll be at his disposal whenever he wants? I'm so confused and thinking is difficult. Or maybe that's just his hands gripping my ass under my dress, pressing my body against his. And it's been a while since I noticed how hard he is.

Is this really happening? God, he tastes so good—like pure sin wrapped in a perfectly tailored shirt and well fitted pants. I love his smell. I think I need to buy his cologne and spray it on my pillow so I can sleep better at night. Whoever I marry one day will *have* to wear this. No question.

And he can kiss... oh, he kisses like a god. I don't think my lips have ever experienced such beautiful flattery. I'm completely blown away.

Alexander pushes the bottom part of my dress up over my thighs, sliding his hands over my sides, back, and stomach. He loosens my belt and sets it aside, then he's able to slip the dress up and off over my body. I break our kiss just long enough to raise my arms and help. Now, sitting in his lap in nothing but white lace panties and a matching bustier with a little bow, I catch his smile before his eyes lock with mine.

"How innocent. I would've guessed black—or maybe floral."

"I didn't want it to show through. The dress turns a bit transparent in sunlight," I admit.

"Yes, I noticed."

"You were watching me?" I ask, surprised.

"All evening," he confesses easily. "I kept imagining your underwear… and how you'd look naked."

"Oh really?" I beam at him. God, I love how confident he is. He says what he thinks, takes what he wants. "And yet you left me hanging. Why didn't you just take me to your room?"

"Because you were pretending to be drunk. Your own fault," he teases.

"I wanted to test you," I admit as he unhooks my bra. Gently, he slides the fabric from my shoulders, baring my breasts—and immediately welcomes them with his lips.

"We men aren't that complicated. Women overthink situations that we're not even aware of," he murmurs while licking and teasing my peaks.

Oh fuck, that feels so good. My back arches, one of his hands pressing me against him while the other grips my breast. With my neck extended, my long hair reaches down to my hips. I gently move my pelvis back and forth to tease him a little. Is it working?

"Are you this greedy, London?" he asks.

Yes. Yes, it worked.

"I want you, Alex," I breathe against his lips, kissing him hungrily as I undo the last buttons of his shirt. He's working at his pants until I stop him.

"I'll handle that," I murmur. I want to unwrap him. My man. My pants. My hard surprise.

First, I undo the last buttons of his shirt while he spreads his arms across the back of the couch. Like a king, he sits there enjoying the little show.

"You have an incredibly beautiful body," he says with an open smile, eyes roaming without shame. My face heat instantly.

"So do you," I reply and open his shirt so I can see his firm chest and toned stomach. Next comes his belt and pants. I wanted to take my time, but I'm hungry. So, I tear open the packaging. Zip. And there it stands before me.

I grin at this beautiful, twitching piece of flesh in front of me, and I immediately grab it with both hands. Alexander takes a deep breath as he watches me. I lean toward him and massage his hardness while gently kissing him at the same time.

"May I?" he asks, as I threaten to take control.

"What do you have in mind?" I ask.

"You'll see," he says and takes back the wheel. He slides my panties aside and presses himself against me, making a moan escape before I can stop it. Fine. He can gladly lead while I enjoy myself. I get it. I wasn't really keen on being in control anyway, even though I usually like to. But if he's the boss—even outside the office—I have absolutely nothing against it.

When he enters me, I gasp at the sudden, delicious surprise, but his strong hand on my back holds me firmly to his chest. With a broad smile, I savor the moment, savor *him* inside me. So forbidden. Indecent. So damn hot.

Who would've thought, or even suspected, that Alex and I would harmonize so well? If it's already working now, will we also be able to work well together?

His deep voice caresses my ear.

Damn, that's hot.

I love hearing him groan. I want to give him more everything to make sure he has a good time. So I give up my body to him so he can experience pure pleasure, while I reap the reward of his body and many orgasms.

Eventually, the couch is a mess, and he carries me to the bedroom where we continue.

I might need to apologize to the neighbors for the noise tomorrow. During another climax, I completely lose control over my voice, and that could certainly irritate some people here in the neighboring apartments.

Eventually, Alex lies on top of me, kissing my neck. I think we're both spent and can't go on but feeling him on me is fantastic. He buries me under his muscles, like a hot blanket.

I trace my fingertips over his sweaty back while he caresses my neck.

We're both exhausted. It was a wild night.

A *damn* wild one...

"Blond, glasses, and a small beer belly," he now whispers in my ear.

I'm caught.

"Why did you tell Stephanie you have a completely different type?"

I knew she'd tell him about that.

"I didn't want her to tell you that I think you're hot. I really couldn't tell your best friend that."

"Hmm, I get it."

"And you're my boss."

"Will be," he corrects me.

"And now it happened." I sigh softly and close my eyes. The small lamp on my bedside table lights up my bedroom. "Do you want another coffee?"

"No." He sounds exhausted.

"Do you want to stay over?"

"Are you trying to kick me out?"

"No." I reach my hand out to turn the lamp off, and the room drowns in darkness. "Today was really beautiful. Work was fun, the summer festival was a complete success, and I saw the starry sky."

"This doesn't even make your top three?" Alex asks me surprised as he lies down on his side.

Bu then he immediately pulls me into his arms so that I can't escape.

"The night was even better than the day. Conversation. Sex. Falling asleep together…"

"That's better."

Maybe I'll wake up tomorrow morning and it will all be just a wild dream. Maybe Alex carried me to my apartment, left immediately, and I've just imagined the last few hours, and it never happened.

When the bright morning comes, I'm alone in my bed.

I knew it.

No Alex. Just the bitter reality.

I sit up, sigh, and glance around. His things are gone too. Of course. A man like him doesn't stick around for breakfast. Yawning, I head to the bathroom to freshen up. I need to properly wake up first. He didn't spare me last night. I grin.

That was definitely an intense workout session.

I walk into the living room in my bathrobe, and it smells like coffee. He must have made some earlier this morning.

I take a look at the couch: every cushion neatly in place. He even tidied up…

Ah. I sigh and wish he'd stayed. Then again—he's my boss. Well, from Monday on.

I shuffle to the coffee maker and turn it off as it's finished brewing. I take out the pot, inhale the aroma, and pour myself a little to taste it. Perfect. Add some milk and sugar, and the morning can begin.

What time is it anyway? I glance at the oven clock: 9:17. That's basically the break of dawn for a Saturday.

Coffee cup in hand, I walk to the coat rack and dig out my phone from my handbag. I return to the couch and set the cup on the table, fishing out my charger from behind a potted plant. I need to charge my phone—it only has four% left. That wouldn't have lasted much longer. I yawn again and take another sip.

Man, I'm worn out.

I smack my lips and can't help a grin.

What a wild night!

I lean back checking my phone. Vanessa has sent me several texts, and other friends have also reached out. There's also one from Alex. A one-time view picture. What's that about? Did he make a mistake?

I open it only to see it's me from early this morning.

Naked.

I gasp and leap up, bumping the coffee table so coffee sloshes over the edge. A few drops spill onto the wood.

"What the...?" I whisper, bewildered. He's added a suggestively grinning emoji. I can't take a screenshot or reopen the image, so I don't close it yet.

Sunlight falls across my body. The blanket lies low on my hips, hiding the lower part of me. One thigh peeks out. The rays of light make my skin glisten. My hair is spread wildly over the pillow, the sheet beneath me completely rumpled.

"That bastard," I mutter in disbelief, pacing my living room. He has a picture of me. Naked! "That asshole!"

Coffee wakes me up but a message like this will keep me awake for three nights.

Although... the photo isn't actually suggestive, but almost artistic. The focus is on my face, not my breasts.

I sit back down, staring at the image. There must be a way to save this. Then I remember the polaroid I still have. Carefully, I set the phone on the table and dig out the camera from the cabinet. Of course, it's at the very bottom and needs a new battery and an empty frame. My hands are shaking like crazy as I finally get it ready.

I lean over the table and photograph the image. Fourteen tries later, I finally get one good enough. Only then do I press the button to return to the chat. The image vanishes. Forever? No—he surely still has it on his phone. He can look at it anytime. And send it to anyone. Oh God.

I need to go to him. Right now! I gulp down the now lukewarm coffee—doesn't matter, it just has to go down. Then I skim through Vanessa's chat, where she's told me all about her breakfast.

I record a voice message for her, since she seems to be doing fine while my life is going down the drain: "Hey, I'll get back to you later. Good morning first of all. Sorry. I'm totally flustered. Umm..." Where was I? Oh, right! "I need to go to Alex. God, if you knew what happened. You'll never believe it. But I'll tell you more when I'm back and I'll have more time. I'll come over to your place." Thankfully, the cable is long enough that I can sit on the couch while my phone charges a little. "I need to shower and then I'll head over there. It's a long story. I think I could be at your place by midday. Around 2? I'll bring something to eat. What are you in the mood for?"

She replies with a flood of question marks and a text in all caps: "WHAT HAPPENED? LONDON? TELL ME!"

By then, I'm already in the shower.

After I've put some clothes on, I rush back to the living room. Vanessa is still buzzing with excitement, demanding: "Don't leave me hanging!"

I record another message while brushing my hair, trying to keep it short: "Hey, I'm back. So, I need to leave right now. I want to go to Alex. We slept together. When I woke up, I thought I'd dreamed it, but no—it really happened. I'm remembering everything better now. I'll tell you more when I come over later. Gotta go now!" I send it off. Damn, only 27% battery. Not much. I need to find my power bank. Wasn't it with the camera? I rummage through the drawer and actually find it. One charge out of three. Well, that should be enough.

I shove everything into my purse and leave my apartment.

Thanks to GPS, I'm in front of Alexander's house in half an hour. It's on a quiet street, lined with villas and single-family houses. Perfectly kept front yards, luxury everywhere. It's immediately noticeable that there's no trash on the street or potholes. This must be a nice place to live.

I find his house and park in the wide driveway. He even has double garage. Is Alex a luxury car guy? Probably.

I need to gather myself before I give him hell.

Okay, stay calm. Everything will be fine. I can handle this.

One last look in the rearview mirror, then I grab my things and step out of the car. I hope he's home, otherwise I don't know what to do with all this anger.

Chapter 20

Alexander

I'm standing in the kitchen when I notice that London has opened the single-view image. A satisfied grin spreads on my face as I turn on the coffee maker. I wonder how she's reacted to it. If only I could see her.

My enjoyment is disturbed, however, as Stephanie starts bombarding me with pictures again. She's been spamming me for days with photos and videos from her honeymoon. There was even a room tour that went on for eleven whole minutes. After that came photos of the beach, the resort, the food, and many selfies in various outfits and bikinis. But one thing is missing: where are the couple photos?

I'd actually wanted to give Marc some peace during his honeymoon, but Stephanie's behavior doesn't entirely sit right with me. So, I text him: *Hey, is everything okay with you and Stephanie? Did you have a fight?*

The pictures make it look as though she's vacationing alone, not honeymooning with the man she loves.

"No, *but she's acting strange,*" Marc replies instantly. Lucky timing—he's on his phone too.

Me: What do you mean? Jet lag?

Marc: No, it's her mood. She doesn't want sex, she's constantly on her phone, we don't even cuddle. She went to see your secretary. I thought they'd cleared everything up?

Me: Yeah, Stephanie is convinced you didn't have an affair. She assured me of that. Maybe the flight threw her off?

Marc: She's cold and distant. Last night she cried, and this morning she was alone on the beach. It doesn't feel like a honeymoon.

Me: Want me to talk to her?

Marc: I'm her husband—that's supposed to be my job. But yes. I need your help. I've already tried, but she keeps avoiding me.

Me: Is she alone right now?

Marc: Yeah, I'm by the pool at our villa, but she's off at the beach somewhere.

Me: She just sent me another picture. I'll call her.

Marc: Whatever this is... I love her. But right now, I don't feel like she loves me. It's so strange. I don't even recognize her anymore.

Me: Anymore?

Marc: This is how she used to be with me, years ago. But after we got together, she was clingy and sweet. What if she regrets the wedding? What if she saw your assistant's interruption as a sign not to marry me?

Me: Something is off, I agree. I'll call her and get back to you right away.

I video call Stephanie because I really want to see her face. It rings only once before she answers.

Her loose hair waves gently in the wind and she wears a shell necklace. She beams at me immediately, seemingly full of joy and happiness, as if everything in her world is perfect.

"Hey, what a coincidence. I was just thinking of you," she says. Behind her, I can see white sand and the deep blue sea. Honestly, I could use a trip there myself.

"You've gotten quite a tan," I start, then admit, "I should fly down there for a weekend and lie on the beach."

"Great idea! Come on over. If you leave now, you'll be here in about eleven hours." She sounds genuinely excited, which makes me laugh—but also confirms Marc's worry. Something's off.

"I can't intrude on your honeymoon," I reply. "But maybe in a few weeks."

"Will you take me with you?" she asks. For a moment, I'm speechless. She's unusually clingy with me.

"You and Marc are both welcome to join," I say, and she seems petrified for a split second. "I mean, if you want to bring your husband, of course."

"Uh, yes. Of course."

"Is everything okay between you two? You should be on cloud nine right now," I ask her directly. This way I don't even have to pretend I don't know anything. "You know you can always talk to me, right?"

Stephanie hesitates, then admits, "The flight was long, I'm exhausted, and Marc constantly wants sex. I just wanted to relax here, enjoy myself. It's... strange. I don't know." She looks sad. Then, almost pleading: "I wish you were here with me instead of him."

She shouldn't be saying things like that.

"Don't you trust him anymore? London's friend Vanessa really didn't have anything with him."

"Yeah, I know. The guy's name is Dominic. She showed me everything—chats, pictures, all sorts of stuff. I believe her." But her expression tells a completely different story.

"What's really going on?" I press.

"I'm just exhausted. The last week was hard. So much has happened, and the weeks before drained me too. I thought I'd recharge and relax here, but instead, we're bickering about everything." She pauses significantly before confessing, "You and I have never argued, Lex. You always get me. You sense when something's wrong immediately. It's like we have this very special connection."

"Yes, like family. Like brother and sister," I cheer her up, which once again leaves Stephanie looking rattled.

Doesn't she like the analogy?

"Yeah. Right. Like brother and sister. The coolest siblings in the world." She lowers her gaze, and suddenly I think I understand what's going on in her head.

"You'll have that with Marc too, eventually. He loves you more than anything, I know he does. Give it time—time for him, for yourself, and for the two of you together. Stay at the beach a while longer, soak up the sun, then go back to him. Talk it out. Communication is everything in a relationship. Especially a marriage."

"Mmh. Yeah, you're right." She looks at me sadly. "I should talk to him. I owe him that."

"You can do this."

"Thanks, Lex. It means so much to me that you're always there for me, that you care."

"Of course. It's an honor. I'll take care of a few errands now. Just let me know if anything comes up, okay?"

"I will." She smiles at me, then hangs up. Maybe they really did rush into this marriage.

Me: *A little tip from me: enjoy the time, give Stephanie her space. The last few weeks have drained her mentally. She needs room. Don't argue over the little things.*

Marc: But she's the one arguing? I was just in the kitchen, she came in and boom, she snaps at me. I hadn't even said anything yet. Her nerves seem really frayed.

Me: She's coming to you now. Hold her tight. Talk to each other. Things will get better.

Marc: From your lips to God's ears.

I fix myself some breakfast—eggs, yogurt, and some nuts. After last night, I need all the energy I can get.

It's a pity that what happened with London was just a one-time thing. I'd very much like a repeat.

I grab my phone and try to reach my housekeeper. It's 9:37. In twenty-three minutes, she should be at my door. In the meantime, I settle in with my laptop in the living room to get some work done. A few messages from employees are waiting. By now, they've all confirmed—they're ready to relocate here. It'll be an expensive move, but worthwhile for all of them. I'll make sure of it. Even the one whose wife was desperate to stay in the U.S. has agreed.

At 10:21, the doorbell rings. I smile. So, she did come after all. Maybe her phone broke down, or there's some other reason my messages didn't get through. There'll surely be a good excuse.

I open the door—only to my surprise, I find London standing there instead of my housekeeper.

"Give me your phone right now!" she snaps, I look past her while she thrusts out her hand in demand.

"You're not my housekeeper," I say, eyeing her skeptically.

"I want your phone!"

"To delete the photo?" I ask with a broad grin. She flushes instantly, then pushes me back into the house. "Is that why you're here?" Her demeanor amuses me.

"What if someone else sees it?"

"Who would I send it to?" I counter, shutting the front door again.

"Your friends. Marc or Stephanie."

"I wasn't planning to."

"Delete it!" she demands, vehemently.

"Or else what?"

She falters for a moment.

"Or else what, London?" I taunt, as she glares at me. "You drove all the way here just to ask me to delete a picture?"

I circle around her, and the goosebumps rising on her arms are impossible to miss. Stopping behind her, I rest a hand against her stomach and press my lips to her neck. With her hair pulled back in a ponytail, there's nothing blocking me.

"I think you're here because you want me to take another picture of you. You, naked in my bed. How does that sound, hm?"

"That's not why I came here. That was a one-time thing."

"I see. As you wish," I murmur with a soft laugh, letting go of her and strolling down the hallway.

"Hey, stop!" she demands, but I don't even think about doing that.

London trails me into the living room, where I drop into the armchair and look at her expectantly.

And now, princess? What's your next move?
I think I'm starting to enjoy teasing her. Still, I can't read her. Did she sleep with me just to soften me up—or is there real desire behind it?

Chapter 21

London

This guy!

"I'm calling your mother," I threaten, which only makes Alex laugh. "She's on my side."

"You want to tell her we had sex, and I took a picture of you? I'd love to witness that conversation." He leans back comfortably, beckoning me with his dominant hand. "Go ahead."

"Don't be so sure I won't." I raise my brows, to threaten him. But unlike me, he's completely calm. I already fear this is a battle I can't win. "I'll do it!" I insist, and frantically dig out my phone, as if I'm about to call. Alexander doesn't even blink. "Just give me your phone so I can delete the picture!"

"Only under two conditions."

Two conditions?

I listen attentively and remain a few steps away from him. But I'm still holding my phone in my hand so he can see it clearly.

"Two conditions?"

He smiles at my question, cold as ice.

"You're going to cheer me up right now, and on Monday we're going to the boxing club together."

"You just want me to go boxing with you?" I'd be there anyway.

"You'll be very nice to me there," he says, grin widening.

"You mean flirt with you in front of the others?"

"No. You'll see."

I swallow. Damn, why does he seem so confident and assertive? What is he up to? He's not going to throw me into the ring or kiss me in front of the men, is he? Nah, he wouldn't do that. Maybe he just wants to be seen with me and train together.

"And how exactly am I supposed to cheer you up now? You're already grinning.." Isn't that enough?

"Do we have a deal? If yes, you'll get my PIN—when we leave the boxing club."

I take a deep breath. "But what should I do now? I'd like to know before I agree."

This is what I get for falling asleep and trusting him.

"I'll leave that up to you."

So it's my choice. I already know what I need to do.

"Okay. Agreed. Deal."

Alex smiles, clearly satisfied, waiting.

I sigh softly and glance down at myself: a simple mint-green summer dress with and elastic waistband and a wavy pattern--looks like someone washed their paint brush in water. Sandals, no jewelry.

Slowly, I lift the hem a bit so I can grab my underwear. I pull it down to my knees before it falls to the floor on its own. I glare at Alex, who is visibly enjoying the little strip show. I sigh then lift the dress over me, taking my sports bra along in one movement so I don't have to take either off completely.

I turn to him, spin around once, giving him a reproachful look, and then get dressed again.

"Hmm. Seen that already," he mocks.

Excuse me? How dare he!

"That's not enough for you?"

"You'll have to come up with something better," he teases me and seems rather bored, though the slight grin remains. He knows exactly how crazy he's driving me. No matter what I do, I'll probably never satisfy him enough to get his PIN.

"Then tell me what you want," I demand.

Alex smiles and pats his thigh three times with his hand, a clear sign for me to come closer. I pull the sports bra and dress back over my body, but he disapproves.

"No. Not like that."

What does he mean?

"Take it off."

"What happened last night was a one-time thing!"

"One time in your apartment," he counters smoothly.

Oh no, he's not getting around it like that. I stand there, not really knowing what to do.

"You can keep the sandals on," he says with a satisfied smile.

I'm afraid he means it. With a grim look, I slip off my dress and bra, then slide out of my panties and push them aside across the floor. I just throw my dress and sports bra on top of them. Annoyed, I put my hands on my hips.

"And now?"

"You could let your hair down," he says and smiles happily.

That too.

I sigh, remove the hair tie, and toss it onto the pile of clothes. Then I run my fingers through my hair to loosen it up.

"And now come over here and take a seat."

"Where exactly?" I ask, because the armchair is next to a couch. He follows my gaze and then brushes his thigh with his hand.

"I'm just supposed to sit down?" Alex smiles at that. "It was a one-time thing, and it will stay that way. I'm definitely not going to start a relationship with my boss!"

"I'm not your boss yet."

I inhale deeply at that. The things we do to get a PIN.

So I step closer and want to sit on his lap, but he makes an instructive gesture with his right hand. I briefly consider what he might mean before I get it and sit on his lap backwards and nestle my back against his chest. Alexander's hands soon wander over my bare stomach to my breasts.

"I'm not completely satisfied yet, but it's not a bad start." He whispers hungrily in my ear, giving me goosebumps.

His deep voice makes me tingle all over.

He reaches for my breasts eagerly, teasing my nipples, then moves both hands down a little. One rests on my stomach, while the other slides between my between my spread legs. I whimper eagerly and place my hands on his wrists. Oh, that's unfair!

"You can look as angry as you want. Your body's telling the truth," he says with a slightly mocking undertone, while I shudder. Alex massages me skillfully, which elicits hot and greedy sounds from me. This is so unfair. I wasn't prepared for this at all

I tilt my head, offering my neck for him to kiss. But suddenly, Alex pulls back, just as I'm getting worked up.

"Don't stop," I plead desperately. That's just cruel.

But then I hear him undoing his belt.

"Please, keep going..." I whimper and gently move my body until I feel his hardness between my legs.

I look down at myself while he presses me against him again with both hands on my stomach. Skillfully, he guides himself into me with one hand, making me moan with satisfaction.

Alexander's hands grasp my breasts, my stomach, my hips, while he simultaneously moves inside me and I rotate my hips. It feels fantastic.

I lean my face closer to him, panting against his cheek, and don't hold back for a second.

"This is so good..." I pant insatiably while enjoying his deep sounds. Hearing how aroused he is and how much fun he's having makes me shudder again.

My body belongs to him. For the second time.

Twice is coincidence, isn't that what they say? Whatever. Just this one more time and then never again. Just now. Just today.

The living room becomes our playground — the armchair, the couch, even the table becomes the perfect place for a wild moment. Alex is so greedy and demanding and demanding that I simply let myself be carried away like a small rowboat on the high seas. The waves will soon crash over me, but I enjoy the ride. Again and again. With each sweet and intense climax comes another, even bigger one that almost takes my breath away.

I'm lying face down on the couch. My butt is sticking up slightly as he kneels behind me and pulls out of me.

I'm completely exhausted and whisper: "If you want to go again, go ahead. But I can't move anymore."

I will never complain about exercising again no matter if it's weightlifting, jogging, or jumping rope. This was much more intense and it came with several rewards that I don't get from exercise. The dopamine and serotonin kicks are really awesome, but they don't hold a candle to orgasms.

Smiling, I lie there trying to catch my breath while he gets up and adjusts himself. Unlike me, he kept most of his clothes on.

And then there's a slap on my ass.

"Hey!" "Hey!" I exclaim in alarm, which makes him laugh. Am I a horse that needs to be patted down after being ridden really hard? Seriously!

"I think I'm quite satisfied. Do you want to join me in the shower?"

"Quite satisfied? Have I fulfilled the first part of the deal now, or not?"

I slowly sit up as he extends his hand. After brief hesitation, I take it. Alex helps me stand up.

"Yes, you have. My bedroom is upstairs. The shower too."

I say seriously.

"Okay," he says rather indifferently.

That bothers me. He's not even fighting for a chance to do it a third time?

"Even though the sex is great, it just can't happen again."

He nods in agreement. "Best sex I've ever had. But yes, it should stay this way. From Monday on, we need to be professional."

Is he serious? He's not even grinning. So, this isn't a joke on his part?

"Do you want to shower alone? I have a guest bathroom down here."

"Yes," I reply, still standing next to him completely naked.

Alex doesn't even look at my breasts anymore as he fastens his pants.

"Okay, make yourself at home. I'll be right back."

His smile seems forced as he leaves. His face neutral, he exits the living room, and I'm left alone.

What was that all about? I'm totally confused.

I pick up a blanket that has slipped to the floor, wrap myself in it, and sit down. I need to process what just happened to me emotionally.

Chapter 22

Alexander

I didn't really want to do this. Truly, I didn't.

Originally, the plan was to annoy her a little and then make her delete the photo, but things got out of hand. Having control over her feels incredibly good. She's just so different from all the other women I've met in my life. Stubborn. Feisty. Calculating?

What is she hoping to gain by sleeping with me? Just a good time, or perhaps a permanent contract that would make it difficult to fire her someday? Right now, it would be easy to let her go during the probation period, but not after that.

I step into the shower and let the warm water run down my body while I think.

Is she after my money? Does she hope for an easier life if we have a relationship? I wish I could see inside her head.

I'll just enjoy whatever comes my way. I still have a few weeks to decide where this journey should go.

With only a towel around my hips, I walk into my bedroom. From here, I can hear the water running in the shower downstairs. So, it will be a while before she's finished.

Marc and Stephanie have both texted me. First, I check Marc's message, then the one from my best friend.

Marc: She just came back and we had a long talk. Thanks for speaking with her, it seems to have done her a lot of good.

Me: Were you able to clear everything up?

Marc: Yes, and now we're enjoying the rest of our honeymoon.

Me: That's great!

Stephanie: You're the best friend I could ever wish for...

Me: I know :)

Stephanie: I'm looking forward to being back in London, but for now, we're still enjoying our honeymoon.

She writes exactly the same thing as Marc. Either they coordinated their messages, or it just shows how similar they are — how perfectly made for each other.

So that's settled.

I put on a well-fitting pair of jeans and a tight shirt, then head downstairs barefoot. It's already 11:17; we were busy for quite a while. Smiling, I stand in the kitchen and start preparing tea. That's a habit I couldn't shake even during my time in the States.

I'm going to cook something. In the last few hours, I gave my muscles a serious workout. Sex really is the best sport in the world.

I marinate a few chicken breasts and set them aside. Then I prepare a salad, cook some rice, steam the broccoli, and bring milk to a boil to make vanilla protein pudding. I'm really in the mood for something sweet after the *workout*.

Just then, I hear the shower turning off.

Chapter 23

London

I'm sitting on the edge of the bathtub, texting Vanessa. She doesn't even know the full story yet, but I'm so frazzled that I can't think clearly anymore.

Me: We just slept together again.

Nessa: Ooh, so now you're officially together?

Me: No idea. It was kind of intense and strange at the same time. He was so dominant, completely different from last night. Yesterday he was considerate and sweet, but now...

Nessa: What exactly do you mean?

Me: Last night it felt almost like... as if he had feelings for me. But now it was just sex.

Nessa: But you don't want him to have feelings for you, right?

Me: I think my hormones are just messing everything up right now. I can't think straight. I'd better head out. I'm still in his bathroom. Just showered. He's in another one.

Nessa: See you soon. I can't wait to hear every little detail!

I let out a quiet sigh and gently towel my hair dry before slipping into the bathrobe that's left here. I should have brought my clothes into the bathroom with me, but instead I only have the blanket. I grab it too as I leave the bathroom.

When I pass the kitchen, I see him standing at the stove. Alex turns toward me and asks, "Did you find everything?"

"Yeah. I'm just getting my things."

If he's already started cooking, then I'd better leave as soon as possible. In the living room, I neatly fold the blanket and place it back on the couch, get dressed, and tie my hair into a loose bun. It's still damp; it'll have to dry without a hairdryer. It's nice and warm outside, so it should dry pretty quickly.

I sneak back to the kitchen. Alex ignores me and calmly continues cooking.

"What is this between us?" The question slips out before I can stop myself. Alexander looks at me briefly, then turns back to his pan.

I lean against the refrigerator, watching him.

"What is this between us?" I didn't actually want to ask him that, but now it's done.

Alexander turns to me curiously then looks back at his pan.

I get closer and lean against the built-in fridge.

"What is this becoming, I mean. Do we have a relationship now? Or was it just a twice-only thing?"

"Do you really want to talk about something like that?" he asks me skeptically.

"I'd rather have your PIN to delete the photo."

"Is that the only reason you're still here?"

Alright, someone clearly wants me to leave.

"Actually, I came about the cleaning job. Since you don't have anyone, I thought I could take it on," I confess to him. "That was the original plan, but then I drove over because I wanted to delete the photo."

"I don't think my housekeeper is coming today. Really a shame. I expected more from her. So, the position is open."

"Would you hire me?" I ask him directly, which leaves him staring at me speechless.

"What? No. Of course not."

"I could really use the money."

Maybe I can convince him with that.

"I don't plan on firing you."

"A little more money would still be good. And I enjoy cleaning. Plus, I can assure you I won't steal any cash or other valuables."

"Hmm," he grunts and gives me a serious look. "Then I'd never get any peace from you."

"You could go somewhere else in the meantime. Meet with friends or have brunch with your parents while I clean here," I offer him.

"You already work hard enough. If you want more money, I'll pay you more. I'd prefer that over you overexerting yourself here. You need time for yourself too."

"And you need a reliable cleaner."

"I'll book one from an agency. *Handy* or something like that. They're in the US too and have been in London for a while now. Very reliable cleaning staff."

""I would have liked to help you. Especially since your trust was betrayed." I mean that sincerely.

"My food is almost ready." I look at the meat he's still cooking; it looks really delicious.

"I promised Vanessa I'd stop by with food. She's waiting for me." I should get going.

"And thanks for the many orgasms." *Now* he smiles.

"All those intense climaxes..." I sigh softly.

"Keep them as a good memory, there won't be more from me." So that's clear. He doesn't want a relationship.

"Damn. And I can't even recommend you to others," I joke, and we both laugh.

"I'll keep quiet about it too."

"And on Monday I'll come get my photo," I playfully threaten, before pointing to the exit. "I should get going now. Thanks for letting me shower here."

"Drive safely. See you Monday. Be on time."

"I always am."

I leave his house and quietly close the door behind me. My legs are still trembling a little as I walk to my car. Once inside, I drive off immediately—but only make it a few streets before I have to stop. My heart is racing, and I'm completely flustered.

Damn it.

Damn it. I think I have feelings for him. Or at the very least, it feels like I'm developing them. It hurt when he let me go. Now I'm sitting here with tears in my eyes, wishing for nothing more than to have accepted his meal invitation.

What if that was his way of testing whether a relationship with me would work? What if he wanted to get to know me better and I just ruined it?

I pull myself together and drive on. I'll discuss everything in detail with Vanessa. There's nothing better than a girls' day with cleaning, eating, and analyzing men.

An hour later, we're sitting on her couch eating Chinese noodles, rice, and vegetables with chicken, beef, and duck. A little bit of everything. Cleaning hasn't even started yet.

"Why didn't you stay?" she asks with her mouth full. Nobody else would understand her, but I can piece the words together while she shovels more food in.

"Well, I wanted to come to you. And it was kind of totally weird. I just didn't want to stay. Actually, I did, but I also sort of didn't." I hang my head.

"Here. Open." She pushes both fortune cookies toward me since I'm already finished, though her appetite seems endless. "Pick one."

Vanessa then sighs. "And I thought I'm the one with problems."

"Yeah, and I've been talking your ear off for an hour."

"It's better than a soap opera. Nobody could make this stuff up. What's that saying? Life is stranger than fiction. Who said that again?"

"Someone wise," I murmur, staring at the two fortune cookies, taking them in my hand and weighing which one appeals to me most. I take the one that sparkles a bit more. At least I think it does. I open the package, break the cookie, and read aloud: "Don't be deceived, the truth will soon come to light."

"Cryptic."

Yep, I can agree with her there.

"What does that even mean?" I ask, baffled.

"That someone in the Chinese fortune cookie factory had a bad day and thought: Yeah, I'll give a hell of a headache to a poor woman whose heart was broken today after she reads this note."

That must be it. I can't help laughing.

"So, I'm being deceived right now, but the truth will come to light. Well, if that refers to Alexander, I wonder what he's deceiving me about." It could be anything. "What if he took the photo through the app when he sent it? Then he wouldn't even have it. What if he's fallen for me? What if he's just using me sexually and will fire me a day before my probation ends?" I take a deep breath. "Then I really will call his mother!"

We both burst out laughing. Yeah, that would be something—talking to her. She'd definitely be on my side. But that's not the point.

"I'm really curious about what he has planned for you on Monday," Vanessa says, raising her eyebrows meaningfully. I sigh. I'd like to know too. Then I push the remaining fortune cookie toward her. She opens it and cackles loudly before reading: "Your ex wants you back. Let him go, it's not a good idea."

That can't really be written there, can it? I take the note in my hand while she curls up on the couch, almost choking on her food.

"You know, I don't usually believe what horoscopes or things like that, but this is really striking. Don't you think?"

, sitting back down. "The other way around wouldn't have made any sense. Must be fate."

Yeah, but a little glimpse into the future isn't the worst thing.

"Do you want a relationship with him?" she asks seriously.

"He has good and bad sides. Hard to say. I barely know him. But looks-wise, and based on what he can do in bed, he's definitely a perfect ten." I gush, even though I didn't mean to.

"You have good and bad sides too. Everyone does. Nobody's perfect. The question is just whether you can live with his."

"I think so."

Hmm. But before I think about that, I'd like to know what's happening on Monday. Then I'll see.

After a wonderful girls' weekend—I spontaneously stayed overnight at her place—I drive back home on Sunday evening. The week was turbulent, and I'm looking forward to a significantly calmer one.

I wake up to my alarm, arrive at work on time, and everything at the office runs smoothly. I bring Alex his coffee, pick up some suits from the cleaners for him, handle a few small matters he needs taken care of, and sort the important issues so he doesn't get overwhelmed in his first week. The less urgent things I redirect to others.

On top of that, his father asked me to send some documents to his home. This way, Alex is unburdened and can focus on the crucial remaining tasks.

Yep, that's part of my job too. I do what I can.

I'm alone during lunch break, and we don't see each other again until after work, since he's tied up in a two-hour meeting.

We meet in the elevator going down.

"What a day," he says with a deep breath. "In the next four to eight weeks, my team will be leaving the States. I need to speak with some real estate agents later so I can quickly and properly accommodate them and their families—children and pets included. For now, they'll be staying in hotels, vacation homes, or rented apartments. I want to offer each of them at least three options for where to move, so they have the perfect start to their new life."

"Can I help with that?" I ask him.

"I was hoping you'd want to," he admits with a smile.

"That's part of my job too. I assist you wherever I can, especially when it comes to taking the load off you or accommodating employees. If you give me the details, I can take care of everything."

"Details?"

"Yes. Who is the employee, who are they bringing with them, what are their expectations? For example, if it's a single man with a dog, I need to check the breed and what problems might arise. Does the animal need quarantine or vaccinations? That can take weeks or months if you don't plan ahead. If there are children, I need to take care of placements—kindergarten, elementary school, and so on. Do they need a house? Do they want a garden? Is one of the women perhaps pregnant? Are there any severe allergies that would make a house in the city, without a garden, better or..."

We arrive at the ground floor.

"I understand. I don't have lists like that. I've always spoken with everyone personally, but I can give you their names and phone numbers."

Alex thinks briefly then says: "Contracts still need to be negotiated. Only when the entire team is set and we know when everyone can come over simultaneously we can get started."

"What's the timeframe?" I ask so I can plan better.

"At least six months. Many have children, or their partners have jobs. I can't bring them over within a few weeks. At the moment, they can still work from the States. I'll probably fly over every few weeks and otherwise stay in touch through video conferences. It's going to be a challenging time." Nevertheless, he smiles enthusiastically.

"You can count on me completely. Rushing things now wouldn't help much. One thing at a time," I say with a broad smile. "I want you to be able to focus on the work. The first few weeks will certainly be tough, but your father will be here now and then, and I've offloaded some tasks to the department heads. They'll manage just fine."

"What would I do without you?" Alex smiles at me before letting me step out of the elevator first. The affectionate way he says it touches me.

"Still upstairs. In the office. Working overtime and despairing," I counter, amused.

We both walk through security with a smirk and leave the building. Our cars are parked right next to each other.

"Shall we meet at the boxing club in a couple hours?" he asks. ""Seven sharp?" He glances at his watch, then at me inquisitively. That's when I notice he's holding his USB stick again. He's even rubbing it with his thumb, which makes him seem a bit nervous.

"That works perfectly." I don't think he has anything devious planned. Today was a good day and we get along splendidly. Today went well, and we got along splendidly. Maybe he just really wants to train with me and enjoys making me panic a little. Who knows?

Alexander nods a quick goodbye and gets into his car. I start my engine and watch him pull out first.

During the drive to my apartment, my mind is racing. I keep imagining what might happen at the boxing club. Alexander surely won't want to fight against me, and sex in the ring while everyone watches? No, that's just my imagination running wild. He didn't make any suggestive comments today. Not even a sweet look. Alex was completely focused on work, and I followed his lead.

Maybe he just wants to train with me and then I'll be allowed to delete the picture. Or does he expect me to let him keep it? As a memento? Have I perhaps bruised his ego because I want him to delete it? Men are so insanely complicated.

Once home, I freshen up, eat some meat, cheese curds, and a banana before packing my gym bag. After that, I even have time to clean my windows—a good warm-up already.

I leave for the boxing club right on time. Even though I'm twenty minutes early, Alexander's car is already there. Trying to get an advantage, huh?

I grab my bag from the back seat and as I walk to the entrance, I see Carlos lighting a cigarette.

"Weren't you planning to quit?" I tease him with a sweet smile.

"Weren't you planning to come every week?" He grins and takes a long drag. I nod and head inside toward the changing rooms.

It's busy tonight. Even Manuela is here—her back is as broad as most of the men's. Impressive.

But no sign of Alexander. He's probably still changing. Must have arrived just before me.

In the women's changing room, I slip into my workout outfit: loose-fitting shorts like the men wear, ending mid-thigh, and a tight top with a bit of cleavage, showing my midriff. Over it, an open training jacket I keep on during breaks—or when there are too many gawkers. With my water bottle, wraps, gloves, and towel, I head into the hall.

I glance around and spot Alexander and Carlos by the punching bags. I'm a bit nervous, I have to admit. Especially when I see Alexander from behind—because now I know what he looks like naked. I take a deep breath and approach them. Alex is also wearing loose shorts that fall almost to his knees, and a loose black muscle shirt. Whew, completely in black. The outfit suits him extremely well. I'm also dressed all in black, but matching outfits wasn't my intention.

"Hey," I greet them both.

Carlos smiles knowingly; I think he knows more than he would ever admit to me.

"Well, I hope you're staying longer today, little one," he says with a slightly scolding look, then grins cheekily.

"I'll do my best," I assure him.

"I'll make sure of that," Alex chimes in and pushes a rope into my hand. "But first, you'll warm up with me."

"Are you challenging me?" I shoot back, trying to sound combative.

"Of course."

Alexander grabs a jump rope of his own and gets into position. I drop my bag on the bench, slip off my training jacket, stretch, then take a few steps and stretch before positioning the jump rope, while Alex does the same. Carlos stands beside us, crossing his arms over his hairy chest—which everyone can admire thanks to his plunging neckline—and cheers us on by clapping his hands.

"Come on. I'll count!" he calls out.

Now it's on between Alex and me. The only thing is, he's never seen me jump rope. At least, not really. Last week I just did some light warm-up jumps, but I'm really good with it.

"Ready?" he asks me and sets his counter to zero. I do the same.

"Two minutes?" I ask him.

"Okay." Alex nods and looks at Carlos, who pulls out his stopwatch.

"Get in position. Three. Two. One. Go!"

We start jumping. . At first I let him think he's in the lead, but after a few seconds, I crank up the speed.

Sure, I'm very skilled at this, but he's also picking up speed. While we're both disciplined and well-trained, this is probably the only challenge I could win. In anything else, I'm physically at a significant disadvantage.

"Thirty seconds left." Carlos counts us down.

Alex is highly concentrated and doesn't let up but I'm not going to make it easy for him!

"Three. Two. One. Stop!"

Alex and I stop immediately. Well, that was a good *warm-up*. We both smile at each other and hand our jump ropes to Carlos. He laughs loudly and says: "402 for you, little one, and 408 for Alex. Narrow win."

"What?" This can't be true! Yeah, okay, I'm a sore loser. I grab Alex's rope, who's standing there with a grin. "You couldn't do that for ten minutes!" I want a rematch.

"No problem."

Alex takes a sip, and I do the same. Carlos resets our ropes to zero. We get into position. The second round begins. Ten minutes. No problem! And if my cheeks burn like fire, I don't care. I will beat him!

Alex and I are standing directly across from each other as the second round begins. I stare at him while he seems focused. Maybe that's his secret. I need to focus on myself, not on him.

"Nine minutes," Carlos calls out.

Phew, I'm pretty out of breath, I have to admit.

"Five!" My lungs are burning.

"Two minutes!"

When will this end? This is what I get for rarely exercising. My only advantage is that I walk so much in high heels, which has trained my calf muscles a bit more. But that's about it.

"Ten seconds!"

It's almost over.

"Three. Two. One. And stop!"

Alex and I stop, breathless, though I take considerably longer than he does to catch my breath.

"1,809 for you, little one, and 2,178 for Alex."

Carlos high-fives Alex, who reaches out his hand with a broad smile. I get a well-meant pat on the shoulder before I raise my fist to Alex, who bumps it with his.

"Not bad," Alex compliments me.

"I'll beat you! I just need to come here more often," I pant.

"That's exactly what I've been saying all along." Carlos laughs and then points to his office. "I'll go take care of paperwork. What else are Mondays good for, huh?" He leaves us and I'm alone with Alex.

"You didn't make it easy for me," he admits and pulls off his shirt.

"Do I get the PIN now?" I ask as I pace around Alex, drink something and wipe the sweat off with my towel.

"No. First, we train."

What is he planning? Does he just want to make me sweat?

Alex takes two padded *boxing pads* and nods at me. "Show me how hard you can hit."

"Kicks too?" I ask him, setting my water bottle aside.

"Can you get that high?" he goads me and holds his hands at chest level.

"Of course." No problem. I wrap the bandages around my hands, then slip on the gloves. "But I won't go easy on you, just so we're clear. If I hurt you, that's your problem."

I want to seem threatening and show him that I know what I'm doing.

"If you give me a few scratches, I'll gladly take them."

"I meant broken bones," I deadpan, not even smiling anymore.

"With those skinny little arms? Hardly." He's teasing me, grinning, only spurring me on more.

First, I want to warm up with some boxing, so I start throwing punches at the pads. I can see Alex tensing his muscles so it's at least taking him some effort to keep me in check. I really let loose and throw in a few kicks, which he catches with ease.

It feels so good to completely exhaust yourself! Wonderful. I haven't had this much fun in ages.

"You've got more in you! Come on. Harder!" he urges me on.

Easy for him to say! I'm running out of breath and my muscles are aching. I feel good and strong, pumped full of endorphins, but my lungs are burning intensely.

"Okay. Break. Drink something."

I stagger back and stand still, catching my breath, then take a few steps.

"Here. Drink." Alex followed his pads set aside. He holds out the water bottle to me. "Is there at least some electrolytes in there?"

"Yeah."

"And did you eat well before working out?"

"Chicken, skyr, and a banana."

"Perfect. I can tell you got more strength. If we train together in the upcoming weeks, you'll get better."

"Can I have the PIN now?" I ask again, draining half the bottle in one go.

"Are you sure you want to earn it already?"

Earn it?

"Or should we train for another half hour? These punching bags need a proper workout."

They hang from the ceiling. I look at them and take a deep breath.

"I think if I imagine they're you, it'll be easier for me to beat the hell out of them."

"Strong words from a woman who's already gasping for air," he teases with a laugh.

This guy...

We keep going. Sometimes he holds the punching bag, sometimes another guy helps us, since I could never catch Alexander's punches and kicks. We both work up a good sweat, and more and more members gather around us. Word must have gotten around that I'm here and someone is getting closer to me than any other guy. That doesn't seem to sit well with everyone. Whenever someone tries to make a move, though, I brush them off.

Is Alex counting on this? Does it turn him on that I only have eyes for him?

"I think that's enough for today," he tell me in front of everyone else.

About twenty men stand around us, having enjoyed the show of him making me sweat properly. Some are training, others just watching while taking a break. A very long break.

"Can't keep up anymore?" I challenge him, even though I'm completely exhausted myself.

"You want another duel?" he asks and a murmur runs through the crowd. "What'll it be?"

"You pick. I'll take on any challenge!"

"Anything?"

"Yes!"

I'll lose, of course, and by a mile, but he would be competing against a woman and would therefore lose face. So, I would emerge as the real winner. I stand there proudly while the crowd laughs and jeers. Alex, however, looks far from intimidated.

"Okay. I accept the challenge."

There's clapping and cheering—it's getting exciting. What will he choose?

I wring my hands looking at him defiantly.

Alex approaches and stands directly opposite me. "I choose... carrying."

"Carrying?" Before I can finish being confused, he grabs me and lifts me up. I don't even have time to react before he throws me over his shoulder.

"Uh!" I groan, as I lie with my stomach on his shoulder, trying to support myself with my hands on his back. "Hey!" I curse annoyed while Alex spins around and twirls me like a trophy.

Of course, our audience absolutely loves it.

"I'd say I've won. I'm taking my prize and I'm going to enjoy it!" Alex sets off taking me with him like a sack of potatoes fresh from the field.

"Put me down right now, you ass!" I continue cursing. I've completely lost my orientation until I see that he's heading for the back rooms.

Wait a minute. What's going on here? Why isn't he putting me down?

And then there's the hooting and snickering of the other members, calling out to him to give me a good fucking.

Oh God. Hey! That's not what I had in mind!

All I can see is that we're going into a hallway, and then the door closes behind us.

"Stop wriggling so much," Alex says as I try to free myself.

Nope, I don't have a chance. He has me way too securely in his grip. I'm literally being carried off. Oh God, this is so embarrassing.

"What are the others supposed to think?" I ask desperately.

A second door closes behind us. Now it's dark. So dark that I can barely see anything. Alex turns on the light as he spins around. I'm a little dizzy, but then he finally puts me down so I can stand on my feet again.

I can finally see where we are: It's a storage closet.

"That I won. And now it's time for you to earn your PIN." Alex grins and places his hand on my jaw. He moves closer, kisses me hungrily, and simultaneously wraps his other arm around my body so I can't escape him.

The storage room is small. It must be only about fifty to sixty square feet. The shelves hold sports equipment: pads in different sizes, bands, and boxing gloves. There are also bottles, towels, and lotions.

So much for him not paying attention to me at work today. He was saving it. For here and now. For this moment.

Chapter 24

Alexander

This wasn't the plan.

I only wanted to train with her and see how she'd react when we weren't at work.

She would have gotten the PIN anyway.

But goddammit, I can't help myself. The moment I saw her in that hot workout outfit, I couldn't think about anything else but grabbing her in front of everyone and claiming her as mine.

I push London against the shelf and close the door behind me. Everything has to happen at once because I can barely control myself anymore. I let go of her just for a brief moment so I can lock the door. I don't need an audience right now.

"You're not seriously planning to do it here and now..." She doesn't get any further. Or rather: I don't let her.

There are other ways she can come.

How did I manage not to fuck her on my desk at the office today? In that tight pencil skirt, those high heels, and the slightly see-through white blouse with the big bow at the collar. Feminine. Sexy. Elegant. She can wear absolutely anything, but I like her best naked and aroused, when the only thing she's has on is smeared lipstick. Thanks to greedy kisses and other things...

I kiss this incredibly arousing woman and push her harder against the shelf behind her. London first puts both hands on my chest before she starts halfheartedly pounding her small fists against it. She couldn't even pop a bubble with that. I know how strong she is and what power lies in those thin little arms when she decides to use it.

Nah, this is more like her desperate attempt to make herself listen to reason. It's probably a faint whisper, and it's now falling completely silent.

Her heart and her arousal are taking over, because suddenly her arms are around my neck and she's kissing me back.

"Should I stop?" I ask provocatively.

Of course, I already know the answer, but her startled look is pure delight.

"Are you nuts?"

I smile triumphantly, spin her around, and grab both her wrists. I make sure she can hold onto one of the upper shelves while pressing my hips against her firm ass. She gasps greedily, though nothing has even happened yet.

"Not here. We can't. What if someone hears us?"

"Nobody needs to hear us. Everyone knows what we're doing back here. Do you want to disappoint them?"

"Oh God…" she breathes desperately.

Oh yes, she knows what's coming. Everyone in the club will stare at her and celebrate me as the king who managed to hook up with her.

She only has to say no, and I'll stop.

"We can still stop," I offer again.

"Shut up!"

I laugh softly and slide my hands over her arms, down her sides, along her hips.

"There's still time. We could sneak out the back and find another boxing club."

"But I don't want you to stop now…"

"You want me to keep talking?"

I tease, running my hands over her stomach, her ribs, and sliding my fingertips under her sports bra. I push the fabric up over her breasts, which I hold, massage, and caress with both hands gladly. Each one a perfect handful, just the way I like it. As if God himself shaped her breasts to fit my hands. Like two puzzle pieces once carved from the same piece.

"Of course not," she utters desperately and leaves it to me to undress her.

That's quickly done. I run my hands down her stomach and grab her workout pants. Together with her panties, I pull both down—just far enough to access everything I want.

"Oh fuck," she moans willingly, making it crystal clear how much she enjoys what I'm doing to her. This time it's different than at her apartment or my house. This time it's quick. Greedy. Wild. As if it were just a meaningless one-night stand.

Nothing more.

Chapter 25

London

It's already over after a minute, maybe two. I can't believe what I've gotten myself into again.

While Alexander gets dressed, I need another moment. My legs are trembling, and I'm glad I can hold onto the shelf for support. That was intense.

I swallow, collect myself, stand up straight, and put my clothes back in place.

"Do I get the PIN now?" I ask, giving him an angry look.

Actually, I'm mad at myself, because I hadn't wanted to do this anymore. I was so proud of holding out all day, and then this...

"Did you only have sex with me to get the PIN?" he asks skeptically.

I stay silent, watching him just as skeptically. Something between us has shifted, but I don't know what. I only know it's no longer casual or comfortable, but... strange. As if we haven't defined what we actually are. Honestly, I don't even know myself.

"What are we?" I ask him directly.

Alexander doesn't answer. He just glances at me briefly and then says: "You'll get it when I'm at my car. My phone's in the locker room."

"And now I get to walk through the gym and face everyone's stares. Unlike you, I'm now a slut and you're the rockstar." I really don't like this. "And I'll have to find a new boxing club."

Such a huge mess.

"Nonsense," he says before I walk out the door and back into the training hall.

Everyone's already standing there like vultures, jeering. But I'm alone, which makes them briefly doubtful. God, these looks are humiliating. I'm dying of shame.

"Ooh, dark look," one says.

"Hey, where's the guy?"
"She probably killed him."
"Is that blood on her hands?"

Their laughter is unbearable, so I grab my stuff and head to the locker room. Just before I enter, I hear Alexander walking in the main hall. He's celebrated. Cheered. Applauded. He's the star. The king. The one who managed to hook up with me.

That's it. I won't get involved with him anymore. What an ass. He's just using me, like all men do. To him, I'm nothing more than a toy, while I was on the verge of losing my heart to him.

Just then, tears well up in my eyes. I cry. Probably because it's too late and I've fallen in love with him. Him of all people.

If only he had stayed in the States…

I wipe my tears, change quickly, and hurry out of the boxing club. The piercing stares of the other men are devastating. I just want to get out of here.

When I reach my car, I wait inside. Since I'm parked only a few yards from Alexander's car, I won't miss him. I pull out my phone and text Vanessa, who fortunately happens to be online.

Me: I hate him!
Nessa: Who? Alex?
Me: Yes, of course!!!
Nessa: What happened?
Me: We were at the boxing club and then he just picked me up and carried me off. Right in front of everyone!
Nessa: Picked you up?
Me: Yes, threw me over his shoulder. He took me into one of the storage rooms and we had sex. Two minutes. At most.
Nessa: Uhhh…
Me: I can never go back there to train. Everyone knows now that he hooked up with me!
Nessa: Oh, I see. So not uhm… more like Ooooh!
Me: Now I'll be known as a slut…
Nessa: Typical. That's what happens immediately if you're a woman while men are praised. I hate that so much.
Me: I guess I'll have to look for a new job. How am I supposed to work with him now?
Nessa: First, calm down. Take a deep breath.
Me: I'm trying. Crap. He's coming. I'll message you later.
Nessa: Just stay calm!

I start the engine and roll down the window.

"Give me your phone," I demand angrily. It's hard to keep my voice even and not yell, though I'd really like to.

Alexander comes over and digs out his phone. With an inquisitive look, he hands it to me.

"2510," he says.

His birthday?

I type in the number, unlock the phone, and start searching while Alexander loads his bag into the car and leans against the driver's side rear door. I can only see him in the side mirror.

His phone is very practical. No unnecessary apps—just banking, email, and messages.

"Where is it?" I ask.

"You'll have to look for it," he teases in an amused tone.

I sigh and open the gallery, and I'm immediately overwhelmed. Pictures of half-naked women everywhere! I roll my eyes and finally find my photo among all the blondes. I tap it, delete it, and empty the trash so he can't restore it. Hopefully, he hasn't saved it anywhere else.

Curious, I open one of the blondes' photos and am stunned when Stephanie smiles back at me from the screen.

Wait a second...

I scroll through the others. It's all Stephanie!

"You miserable jerk!" I curse, storming out of the car.

Alexander looks irritated and apparently has no idea what's going on.

I shove the phone at him and snap: "She's married, and you're having an affair with her?"

"What?" Alex furrows his brow and looks at the photo of Stephanie still on display. "That's just Stephanie. She's always sending me pictures and videos of herself."

"Half-naked? In a bikini? At the beach? In yoga pants?"

"Yes." Alex's tone is dry and perplexed, which takes the wind out of my sails. Either there really is nothing to it, or he's so jaded that he doesn't even care.

"Did you have those pictures just to make me jealous?" I ask, upset.

"What? No. That's just my main photo gallery—it saves all the photos that are sent to me. Why would I want to make you jealous?" He says it so dryly and casually that it stabs at my heart. I swallow hard and take a deep breath.

"That's not normal. Honestly."

I hand his phone back and move to get in my car.

"She used to do it only occasionally, but shortly before the wedding she started bombarding me with them. I assume she was a bit insecure about whether she was good enough. But what can I say? She is pretty."

Alex sounds a little lost, so I hesitate instead of storming off.

"No woman would send those kinds of pictures if she wasn't interested," I say firmly.

"She got married. Don't you remember? You happened to be there too." Alex doesn't seem interested at all. "We've known each other since forever and there was never anything between us. And now she's married."

"And if she wasn't married?" I ask. My heart beats faster. Is he secretly in love with her?

"Nothing would happen then either. She's just not my type. Even before, she was more like a little sister to me." He says it so indifferently that I almost believe him. But then he grins and asks: "*Are* you jealous?"

"This ends now, Alex. I'm never sleeping with you again, is that clear? I want to do my job, and I want to do it well. Do you understand that? I need this job. Unlike you, I can't afford to be unemployed. Getting into bed with you was a stupid idea. Today was the last time. Please, let's just keep this professional. You're my boss. I'm your assistant. Nothing more." Saying it hurts terribly. So much that tears spring to my eyes again. "Okay? Can you please treat me fairly when we're at work tomorrow?"

I think Alexander finally realizes I'm serious.

"Of course." He straightens and looks thoughtful.

"Thank you." I take a deep breath and open the car door wider so I can get in. The engine is still running, so I only need to close the door and fasten my seatbelt. Alexander steps aside to let me drive away and only then do I allow myself to cry again.

No—this feels wrong. But just because my heart feels this way doesn't mean it's right. I need to listen to my head, and it's telling me to drive home. Alone.

Once in my apartment, I immediately call Vanessa. We still have quite a lot to discuss.

"I'm so glad I can talk to you about this," I sob, curling up on the couch under a blanket. Even though it's far too warm, it feels like it's hugging me.

"What will you do if things get awkward at work?" she asks.

"I should probably start looking for a new job now," I admit. "This is only going to cause problems; I can feel it. And the probation period isn't long. He could fire me any day."

"How much have you saved?"

"Enough. I could live off my savings for two or three years, but that's not what they're for." I sigh. "I'd better start looking at job listings now. It's always smart to have a Plan B."

"Sad but true. But hey, look at it this way: You're damn good at your job, and in an interview, you can easily explain why you want to leave. The old boss was great, but his son unfortunately isn't. If it were still your old boss, it probably wouldn't sound convincing. But thanks to the change, I think your explanation makes perfect sense."

"Yes, you're right." I pull my laptop out from under the coffee table and open it. "I'll get back to you when I find something good."

"And if anything else comes up, call me, okay? Or text."

"I will, I promise."

Without Vanessa, I would be completely helpless and lost. She's the only one I can talk to about these things.

I spend the entire evening searching through companies. As it turns out, there are four current openings that might work. One pays less, but it's close to where I live and the hours are good. Two are similar to my current position, and the fourth pays significantly more but also demands much more work.

On impulse, I update my application documents and submit them to all four companies just after midnight.

I feel much better now.

After that, I go to bed. The day has been long enough, and I've cried twice. Probably just because it's Monday.

Has anything good ever happened on a Monday?

The next morning, I arrive at the office a little earlier. When Alexander comes in, everything feels calm, polite, and formal. We greet each other, I bring him coffee and sort his documents. There's no sign of yesterday in his behavior, which reassures me at first.

The day passes smoothly. I spend lunch alone, and in the late afternoon Mr. Blackthorn Senior stops by for a few meetings with the department heads.

Since I'm on my phone, I check my emails occasionally. No replies yet, but I don't want to stress myself about it.

The days pass, and by the end of the week there's still no response. But things between Alexander and me remain calm and professional. I've already helped him several times and started organizing apartments and houses for his employees from the States. The lists are ready, so I'm in contact with each of them and now know exactly what they're looking for. Handling all of this is genuinely fun, and even Alexander has had nothing but praise. His employees have already spoken positively about me, saying how well cared for they feel—well, that's nice to hear.

"Ah, that would be wonderful," says one of the programmers I'm in touch with because of her dog. "And I was already thinking he'd have to be in quarantine for weeks." She breathes a sigh of relief.

"No, it won't take long—just a few hours, as long as all the documents are ready." I'm genuinely happy for her.

"My husband and I have already looked at the options you found for us, and we're thrilled. Also, a little scared and nervous, but really thrilled. It's going to change a lot and turn our lives upside down, but..." She hesitates briefly. "Did you know that none of us on the team have ever worked at a big company?"

"What? No." Actually, I don't know much about them in terms of work or positions—just what they've shared about their family and living situations so I could find and suggest suitable properties.

"Alex gave us all a chance. At first, we didn't even know he was so wealthy. We thought we'd get a small salary at most. If anything. But then he revealed to us that we were earning good money. At first, we thought it was a bad joke."

"Why didn't he just be upfront from the start?" I ask, surprised by his behavior.

"He wanted us to join because of his idea, not the money. He has a vision, and we're making it happen together. Alex is really an amazing person. And a great boss. I couldn't imagine a better one. That's why my husband and I said yes. London will be a big adjustment, but we're on board. Do you have any idea when we should give notice on our apartment?"

"It will be a little while. Probably three months at least because everything has to be organized thoroughly first. Alex doesn't want to rush anything—he wants to make sure everyone is on the right path first."

She's really raving about him. I'm glad to hear he's made such a good impression.

"Okay, then we'll just wait a bit longer. You'll let us know as soon as there's any news, right?"

"Of course! I'll keep you all regularly updated. Don't worry." I've got that covered.

Two weeks have now passed. Two weeks during which Alexander has been my boss. He hasn't made a single hint, flirted, or given me strange looks. We have a completely normal relationship between a boss and a PA.

Just as I'm about to finish work for the day, a message from Stephanie comes in. I read it, curious:

"Hey, we landed this afternoon. Phew, what a long flight! I'm totally excited to be back in London—I've missed the cold, miserable weather a bit, if I'm being honest. And the good food, of course." She adds a bunch of laughing emojis. *"Would you like to meet up this weekend? I'm sure lots of exciting things have happened in your life? What do you think about cooking together again? That was really fun."*

Now I'm facing a dilemma.

The question is: why is she doing this? Why is she *really* doing this? Pure politeness?

Genuine interest in me as a person?

Or does she want to pump me for information?

I have to remember she's Alexander's best friend. Still... the pictures she sent him tell a different story in my opinion. Maybe I'm just over-thinking. After all, Alexander did say she was only like a little sister to him.

I sigh. It doesn't matter now, anyway. Alex is and remains my boss—at least for as long as I'm still working here.

I shut down my computer and pack up my handbag, when suddenly a young man approaches me.

Who is that?

I stand up and address him immediately. "Hi, can I help you?" I ask.

Probably a friend of Alexander's, since he doesn't have an appointment that I know of. I just hope it's not—

"Marc. Hey. You must be London?"

Damn. I take a deep breath and smile playfully at him. Him of all people. Well, it was obvious that I would run into him sooner or later.

"Hi, yes. It's so nice to finally meet you in person," I babble, extending my hand while he opens his arms to hug me. So, now I try to hug him, but he offers his hand.

We both laugh and finally embrace warmly.

"So, you're really not mad at me anymore?" I ask, a little uncertain.

Marc shakes his head as we pull apart. He looks exhausted—surely from the long flight.

"Everything's fine, really."

"I'm sure you want to see Alex?"

"Yes."

"What can I get you to drink? Coffee, Coke, tea?" I step aside so we can walk down the hallway.

"I wasn't planning to stay long since we're going out tonight. But... a Coke would be great."

"I'll bring it right away." I knock on Alex's door, wait, then open it after hearing a "Come in."

"Your visitor is here." He hadn't told me anything about this. Alex should know how uncomfortable this whole situation still makes me—but he probably didn't think twice about it. "Would you like anything else to drink? Otherwise, I'm about to finish for the day."

"Nothing for me, thanks. What about you, Marc?"

"Yeah, I've already placed my order."

The two men hug warmly while I leave the office. Better get moving. I go to the kitchen, open a small bottle of Coke, and pour it into a glass with a few ice cubes—that's how it tastes best. Carrying it on a small tray, I return, knock again, and only enter after another "Come in."

Alexander and Marc are standing at his desk, laughing and chatting. Alex is holding his beloved USB drive, looking very proud of it.

"This is the key to success. It's finally finished! I'm about to close my first deal with this! The first offer is already at twenty million dollars!" Alex gloats, barely able to contain his happiness.

Well, that's good news—even if I have absolutely no idea what exactly he's created. I'm just glad I don't have to deal with it.

Alexander's phone rings. He looks at the screen, grins, and says, "I need to take this." He holds the drive up to Marc again, which makes them both grin, then sets it down on the desk.

"Here you go, your Coke," I say, setting the tray on the desk. Marc takes the glass and raises it in a toast to me.

"Thank you so much, I'm quite thirsty," he tells me quietly, with a polite smile, while Alexander steps away to take the call undisturbed.

"You're welcome. You can just leave the glass here—the cleaning staff will take it back to the kitchen when they clean later," I answer just as quietly.

"Perfect, thank you."

"Have a nice weekend," I say in farewell, though Alexander pays me no attention at all.

"You too," Marc replies, then leans against the desk. Alexander is now at the far end of the room, his phone call clearly is important. I'm really glad I don't have responsibilities like his. I'm more than satisfied with my job and completely fulfilled.

I drive home and treat myself to fast food on the way. I should really go to the gym, since I promised myself I'd turn my life around—but it's okay every now and then to indulge in burgers and fries.

Sitting on the couch, enjoying the greasy food, I can't help but miss good sex and intense orgasms. I sigh quietly and install a few dating apps. It's time to go on some dates. I can't keep hiding away forever or hoping Alex will come to his senses and something might still happen between us.

Stephanie texts me again: "*So, what's up? If you don't have time, just let me know :)*"

Oh right, there was that too.

"*Hey, I'd love to. When does it work for you? I'm home Saturday and Sunday,*" I text back. I'm meeting Vanessa then too, but I could cook something with Stephanie beforehand.

"How about tonight?"

What? Now?

I'm still eating my burger and I'm almost full, but if she's so desperate to meet, she probably has something else she wants to discuss.

"I've already eaten, but if you want to come by for tea or snacks, you're always welcome," I write back.

"Perfect. I'll be there in thirty minutes," she answers.

Well, that's quite surprising.

I immediately shove the rest of the burger into my mouth and rush to take a shower. Then, I hurry through the apartment, trying to tidy up a bit.

Only twenty-six minutes later, she rings my doorbell.

Wow, this is definitely not how I imagined spending my evening.

I decided on white leggings with a loose pink top. Comfortable. When I open the door for Stephanie, she immediately throws her arms around me like we're best friends.

"Oh, how lovely to see you again," she says happily. Well, I can't be mad at her now. "Look what I brought," she adds, holding up a patisserie box filled with macarons, petits fours, and truffle pralines.

Not bad.

"Well, anyone who brings such delicious things is always welcome in my apartment," I say and let her in.

"Hmm, smells like fast food," she remarks, looking me up and down. "I thought you'd eat more healthily?" I'll take that as a regular question rather than an attack.

"Usually I do, but today was an exception," I admit. Stephanie, of course, is dressed to the nines as always: white pencil skirt, white high heels, a black blouse, a white jacket, and gold jewelry. She always looks flawless.

She slips off her heels at the door, then follows me into the living room where she sets the delicious treats in their pretty packaging on the table.

"Tea?"

"Yes, please. Do you have strawberry or peach?"

"Yes," I reply, putting the kettle on. "Are all of these vegan?"

"Half of them are, the other half aren't. I admit, the vegan ones taste different, not everyone likes them."

How thoughtful of her!

I sit with Stephanie, who seems unusually keyed up.

"So, tell me. How was your honeymoon?" I ask, pushing aside the images in my head of those photos she sent to Alex. I really don't want to think about that right now.

"Oh, it was great. But I'm much more interested in how things went with you and Alex."

What?

I'm surprised she cuts her honeymoon story so short. So, she *is* here to pump me for information. But did Alex send her or is she just curious? I'm not sure.

"Well, we're working together as usual. Marc was there today and..."

"At the office?" she interrupts me. Stephanie looks both shocked and agitated, which makes me suspicious.

"Yeah, they wanted to talk," I say quickly.

Why doesn't she know about this?

"About what?" She's acting so conspicuously that I don't feel comfortable telling her more.

"I was done with work and left them alone. They were in Alexander's office."

"Oh, I see." Stephanie stares off, then quickly grabs the pralines. "Here, try one."

Her hands are trembling.

"Gladly. Thank you." I take one, then ask, "Is everything okay with you?"

The water is done boiling, so I get up and head into the kitchen to pour two cups.

"Yes... yes, um..." She suddenly jumps up. "I just received an important message and unfortunately have to leave already."

"What?" I stare at her in astonishment. Her bag—with her phone still inside—since she's not holding one—is hanging on the coat rack.

"Yes, it's really important. Sorry. You can keep everything, of course. Enjoy!"

She rushes to the door, slips into her heels, and grabs her handbag. Before I can say anything, she's already out the door.

"Okay, thanks. Um. Well, if you..."

"See you soon!" And she's gone.

Okay? What was that about?

I stand in the doorway baffled, peering out into the hallway. Stephanie runs to the elevator—then changes her mind and takes the stairs instead. Someone's in a real hurry.

"And she just ran off?" Vanessa asks, puzzled, as I sit on her couch and we share the pralines.

"Yeah, as if she was completely shocked that Marc had talked to Alex. I mean, those two are best friends. Of course they talk to each other."

"That is really strange," says Vanessa, taking one of the macarons. "God, these are delicious—even the vegan ones. They're just a bit firmer, but otherwise? Absolutely amazing."

"Yeah, I agree... that it's strange. And that those are delicious."

What could that mean?

"What if you tell Alex about it?"

"I shouldn't get involved," I answer.

"Probably better that way."

Yes. Indeed.

Chapter 26

Alexander

I treat myself to a good whiskey in the club's lounge. There are many men here tonight—familiar faces not just from the media, but also from the real estate and corporate sectors.

Cornelius Grey has surely founded a very exclusive club here. I've already had several interesting conversations and made some good networking. Coming tonight was a good idea—especially since I got my eye on one of the servers, whose hip swaying is extraordinarily appealing.

"*Mariella*," says a voice next to me. I glance over and see a man I don't know. I'd guess he's in his late thirties, early forties. "She's a real wildcat in bed and is up for a lot." He sits down beside me and raises his glass in a toast. "But with the right tip, she can be tamed."

I lift my glass too, but I don't comment on his remark.

"Alexander Blackthorn, right?"

"And who do I have the honor of speaking with?" I shoot back immediately.

His cold smile makes it obvious he's a very stern man, and probably not here just for pleasure.

"Matthias Volt," he answers curtly. The name, of course, rings a bell right away—the owner of Volt Security himself.

"Out without security?"

"They're waiting downstairs," he replies. "It definitely has its advantages not always being in the spotlight."

True.

I'd never actually known what he looked like. Dark hair slicked back, sharp cheekbones, clean-shaven, dark eyes. His hands look strong, and his gaze is icy. I once heard he has ties to various mafia organizations. Probably necessary if you're in the security business.

"I'm not approaching you entirely without ulterior motives," he says.

"I figured as much," I reply. Hopefully he's not about to try and sell me bodyguards. I've never needed them, not even back in the States.

"How satisfied are you with London Waverley?" I'm genuinely taken aback when he mentions her name.

"Why do you ask?" I ask.

Why is he of all people bringing up London?

"Because she applied for a position with me." He laughs and adds, "Judging from the look on your face, you didn't know that."

"She's my PA," I answer curtly, buying myself some time to think. "When did she apply? She's still in her probation period."

"She worked for your father for three years before that, didn't she?"

"Correct. But after the change in ownership, she signed a new contract."

"Doesn't sound too good. So, your father wasn't happy with her?"

"Not at all. She's outstanding."

"And yet she applied to me two weeks ago."

Two weeks ago? That must've been the very evening we were at the boxing club.

"I like her. I wouldn't mind having an attractive assistant at my side, who serves me in all aspects of life. She's surely open for that, isn't she?"

"She'll soon be getting a permanent contract with a raise, since I have no intention of letting her go."

"She seemed very serious about her application, and she didn't strike me as someone who wants to stay with you."

I don't like this.

"I'll talk to her."

"Not a good idea. You surely know that everything discussed here in the club must remain between us?" He smiles mysteriously.

"So, you only approached me to tell me that I've lost her?"

He smiles coldly and then stands up.

"Here's a small olive branch: I'll be interviewing her next Friday. You can sit in."

I rise as well.

"And why would I do that?"

"I work with many entrepreneurs whom I bring in as advisors for important conversations. And someone with your experience could certainly be useful to me in figuring out how serious she is about the new job."

My brow furrows. What the hell is this guy up to?

"This is a purely friendly offer. I could've kept it to myself, but I think we men need to stick together." He chuckles and clinks his glass against mine. "Besides, I saw your face. You're jealous. So, she means something to you." He hands me his card. "Reach out Friday. I'll give you the time and place I'm meeting her."

Before I can respond, he walks away and leaves me standing there. But even if he had stayed, I wouldn't know what to say.

A truly lucrative tempting offer. But that's how it is when you deal with the devil—his offers are always enticing. The price you end up paying for your greed, though, may be far too high.

That evening, I use my father's limo service since I've had one too many whiskeys and don't trust myself to drive. The soundproof partition is up, so the driver can't overhear while I talk to Marc on the phone.

"So, what do you think?" I ask him.

"Honestly? Fire her. Immediately." Harsh words from my best friend. "You need employees who are loyal, and she clearly isn't."

"Mh ..." I start pondering.

"Have you thought about my offer?" he asks.

"I have. It would actually make a lot of things easier, and I'd really like to move back to the States." I take a deep breath.

"I'd find another PA if I get your position."

It would be perfect—I could live and work in the U.S. again, my entire team wouldn't have to relocate, and Marc would finally get the chance to run a big company under my supervision. I'd just have to fly to London once a month to handle the most important matters.

"Actually, you need her. London does an excellent job. If you take over, it's only under the condition that she stays."

"Okay. If that's what you want, I agree to that."

That was quick.

"I'll meet with my team a week from Monday, but first I need to talk to London."

"You really want to go through with this? Just offer her a raise and tell her you're leaving. I think she only applied somewhere else because she doesn't want to work with you anymore. If you tell her you're moving back to the States, she'll probably be happy to stay."

"And you'd be fine working with her?"

"Of course."

"A minute ago you wanted me to fire her."

"Yeah, because I thought you weren't okay with her applying elsewhere. But if you're fine with it, then so am I."

Very accommodating of him. Stephanie calls me. Now, of all times.

"Okay, I'm almost home. We'll talk again next week. I'll be in touch."

"Alright. Bye."

Now I can take Stephanie's call. I'm really not in the headspace for this, but she's tried several times today, and I've ignored her every time.

"Hey, sorry. I've been out all day," I answer.

"Oh man, finally..." she complains, but then says: "It's good to hear your voice. Phew. I really need to tell you something." She sounds completely distraught, sobbing and crying.

"Hey, what's going on?" I can't remember the last time I heard her cry. It must have been when we were kids.

"Marc said that he has more important things to do now than take care of his family. The company comes first. He really wants your job."

"I know. I've offered it to him and he's considering accepting it."

"But... I'm pregnant." She cries bitterly.

"You're pregnant?"

Usually good news, but seeing how desperate she sounds, I probably shouldn't congratulate her.

"Please. You need to stay, Alex. Don't leave me alone now, please!"

"Why would Marc not have time for you anymore? Does he know you're pregnant?"

"Yes, but he doesn't care. He just wants to bury himself in work. Please... if you stay, if he doesn't get the position, then... then we still have a chance. I think our marriage is already doomed!"

"Take it easy. I think Marc just phrased things poorly. Of course it will take time for him to prepare for the position, but he'll always take care of you. He loves you. I know that. One hundred percent."

"I need you here in London," she whispers, choked with tears.

"I can't promise that, Stephanie." I need to think about myself and my future. "You're married, expecting a child. He doesn't want this career just for himself, but for you too. Marc told me very clearly he wants to impress you with it."

"I can't make it here without you, Alex."

I can barely understand her anymore.

"Please calm down first, okay? I haven't decided anything yet." If she gets too upset, it could be bad for her. "It was just an idea, nothing more."

"Please stay. Promise me!"

"I'll stay for now. Promise. Nothing's in writing yet. It will certainly take a few months until we've agreed on everything and finish planning.

"When will we see each other again?" she asks.

"Soon. There's a lot going on right now. But I'll come to your place next weekend. Marc wanted to fire up the grill. Doesn't that sound good?"

Maybe that will cheer her up.

"I could come by for a visit? Last time we had lunch together was really nice, wasn't it?"

Yep, those are hormones. Definitely.

"I always have time for you."

"Then I'll come by on Monday." Just like that, her tears dry.
"Okay. Then Monday. 12:30?"
"Yeah, I'm looking forward to it!"
Everything's fine again.
"I'm home now. See you Monday."
"Great! See you Monday!"
There's no trace of crying in her voice now.

That's settled. But I should talk to Marc. Why on earth would he want to leave Stephanie alone during her pregnancy? This isn't like him at all. I hope the prospect of the new position isn't going to his head. That's not what I want, and not what my father would approve of either. After all, it will take quite a bit of persuasion from both of us to convince my father that Marc is a worthy successor.

After the driver drops me off, I call Marc again while I prepare myself a cup of tea since I can't go to sleep just yet.

"Hey, forget something?" he says.
"Yes, actually. Where are you right now?"
"Still out."
"Stephanie just called me. Should I offer congratulations?"
"Yes, of course..."

A father-to-be should sound more excited than this. The two of them are clearly fighting. Let's see if I can help, even if I probably shouldn't.

"What's going on with you two?"
"What do you mean?"
"She's pregnant. You're going to be a father. Neither of you sounds happy."
"It's complicated, but it'll work out."
"Can I help?"
"No, we'll manage. But thanks." Marc sounds exhausted and distant. This isn't like him at all. There really seems to be something seriously wrong between them.

"Stephanie sounded very upset."
"You don't need to worry. It's just hormones," he assures me. "I'll be home soon, then I'll take care of her."
"Okay. But if anything's wrong, you'll let me know?"
"I will."

I sit in my living room until late, drinking tea, and reading. What a mess.

Back in the States, life wasn't nearly this stressful.

On Monday, I head to the office as usual. London sits at her desk, greets me warmly, and immediately offers me coffee.

Sitting at my desk, I sort through documents then unlock the safe. Inside lies the USB drive—my key to success. This software will revolutionize the tech world. This is what I've been working on all these years!

I look at this small, inconspicuous item and plug it into the laptop. I want to grant myself one more test phase before I join the group call with my team. But when I insert the drive, it's empty. No data found. What the hell?

I pull it out, plug it back in. Still nothing. Maybe the laptop is defective? I try another. Then my tablet, with an adapter. But the drive seems to be empty!

This USB drive looks very similar to mine. Only someone who knows me well would know that I use this brand.

I suspect that someone has stolen it. I slowly sit down, look at the empty device, and start to ponder. The data was still there on Friday. Of course, the stick only contains copies—but even those are enough to satisfy the competition. Another company similar to mine would easily pay twenty-thirty million for it.

The only question is who had the opportunity to get hold of the stick. I try to remember when I last used it: it was shortly before Marc arrived. I showed him the stick, put it on the table, and made a phone call.

But what happened then?

There's a knock at the door. "Come in," I call.

London enters and sets my coffee on the desk.

"Do you need anything else?" she asks.

In that instant, it clicks. It could only have been her.

"No. Thank you very much." I observe her. She nods politely and leaves.

She betrayed me. She took a copy of the software and all my data. That's why she's looking for a new job. That's why she wants to leave.

Is that why she also wanted to clean my place? So she could snoop around my home?

I breathe deeply and try to stay calm. If I act hastily now, I won't get the information I need. She must have kept the USB drive in a safe place or has already sold it. I have no evidence whatsoever.

Well, *not yet* anyway.

Chapter 27

London

The week is extremely strange.

Alexander seems very cold and distant. On top of that, Stephanie is here every afternoon, briefly greeting me before disappearing cheerfully into Alexander's office.

I fear the worst...

I suspect the two of them are having an affair.

And yes, I'm jealous. Angry. Hurt.

I'd love to interfere, storm into his office and tell him what a miserable cheater he is. She's married! To his best friend! Couldn't he have chosen Stephanie before she got married? And what was I then? Just a replacement? A temporary solution? A convenient opportunity?

Did I just imagine everything? What about the trip to the field, with the starry sky? No one has ever done anything so romantic for me before...

My probation ends next week, and I haven't received an offer for a contract yet. Not even a discussion.

It's good that I have plans with Mr. Volt tonight. If the conversation goes well, I'll be able to resign next week to start my job there.

Maybe that's why Stephanie is here? Is she supposed to take my place? That would make sense.

I stop by Alexander's office before leaving. "Need anything else before I go?"

"Thanks, no. I have everything. You can leave." He smiles faintly. "Have a nice evening."

"Thanks, you too." That's all. My heart breaks. But maybe I needed this to be able to leave. I mean, to actually leave. Not just for the evening, but forever.

I wander into the kitchen, look around, and get a bit nostalgic. The melancholy hits me harder than I thought, but that's just how it is. And this is only the kitchen...

When I return to my desk, it hurts to shut down the computer and switch the phone to the main center. I'll be back on Monday, but the thought that this will be my last week weighs heavily.

I take the elevator down, say goodbye to the security team for the weekend, and then get into my car.

Mr. Volt sent me an email earlier with specific instructions about when and where our meeting will take place. He warned me in advance that it wouldn't be at his company, but probably in a restaurant. He wrote that he likes to handle such conversations somewhere pleasant. I sincerely hope he's not going to hit on me. It would be really nice if I was hired based on my skills, and not because I'm expected to be constantly available for sex.

When I get home, I open the email that arrived just minutes before. It states exactly what to do:

- Choose an elegant evening outfit. Preferably black or red, long and feminine, not too revealing.

He also sends me the address of a well-known upscale restaurant downtown. He explains that I should ask for him at reception, and the staff would then lead me to the reserved table.

It would be very good if I arrived at exactly 9.

Since I assume punctuality is very important to him, I'm careful not to arrive too early.

"Turn around," Vanessa says during our video call. It's only 7, but of course I want to look perfect and be on time. I still haven't found the ideal dress.

"Isn't red too flashy? I don't know... I'd prefer the black one."

The red feels too bright, the burgundy too somber. The black is timeless, classic. "I'll try on the black dress again."

"Yes, show me again. I need to see the comparison."

I dash out of the frame, toss the red gown onto the bed, and slip back into the black one. It has a beautiful sweetheart neckline, off-the-shoulder cut, and a tailored waist. It's full skirt that makes a striking impression.

"I thought I could put my hair up," I say, gathering it into a bun.

"No, wear it down. With your hair up, you look too severe—and too old."

"I'd rather meet him in his office. Skirt, blouse, blazer. Simple. Does it really have to be in such a fancy restaurant?"

I don't feel entirely comfortable with where this meeting is taking place.

"As a PA, he might be testing how far you'll go—if you're presentable, if you have good manners, that kind of thing," she says, raising her orange juice in a toast.

"Okay. Hair down. Gold jewelry? What do you think?" I hold up a necklace and earrings.

"Oh yes, I like those."

"And this bag?" I show her a black clutch with a gold emblem.

"Yes, I like that too. Add blood-red lipstick and a little eyeliner."

"Red lipstick? I don't know..."

"With a black dress, it's an absolute MUST!"

If she insists, fine. I try it on, fix my hair, fasten the necklace, and slip in the earrings.

"Well?" I turn back and forth until I see her grin.

"That's it. Perfect!"

If she's this thrilled, then surely Mr. Volt will be impressed too.

I take a taxi to the restaurant. I could drive myself, but I'm far too nervous and don't want to risk an accident. This way I can also text Vanessa and let her distract me a bit.

Nessa: And what will you do if he wants something from you?

Me: Look for another job. I'm not going through that again.

Nessa: And what if he's hot?

Me: Doesn't matter. I just want to do a good job. *And meet someone in a different setting.* That thing with Alex was stupid—my fault. Why did I develop feelings for him? Oh well...

Nessa: What if he wanted everyone at the boxing club to know you belonged to him?

Me: What do you mean?

Nessa: *Well, you're pretty desirable there, but now that he's hooked up with you, the others know you're his and leave you alone. This way you can train there without anyone hitting on you senselessly.*

Me: I don't know if that was his intention...

Nessa: In my head it makes sense :)

Me: Many things make sense in your head, my dear ;) I'm here now. Wish me luck!

She hearts my last message just as the driver stops. I had him circle the block so I wouldn't arrive too early.

I pay and get out. After the meeting, I'll head back home, then straight to Vanessa's to spend the night there.

I walk toward the impressive entrance guarded by security. Not everyone gets here. Being under their eyes makes me nervous.

At the reception, I check in: "Good evening. London Waverley. I have an appointment with Mr. Volt." I glance at my watch: six minutes left. "I need to be at his table at 9:00 sharp. How long will it take to get there?"

The young man looks surprised, checks his book, and finds my name. "Ah yes, here you are. Good evening, Miss Waverley. Mr. Volt is already expecting you." He pauses, then adds: "The table is in our lounge. At most twenty seconds away."

I glance at my gold wristwatch. It looks nice though it only cost eighty pounds in a sale. Such a steal!

"Can we see the table from here?" I ask.

"No, it's further back in a separate room."

"Is there a door?"

"Yes, Miss Waverley."

Perfect.

"Then please take me there. I'll wait outside so I can knock exactly at 9:00." He looks puzzled.

"Mr. Volt insists on it."

By the time I've explained, the six minutes are nearly gone and I'll be late.

"I understand. Please follow me."

I nod and walk behind him. He's careful to make sure I don't have to rush.

We pass several set tables. The women are all dressed up and the servers take their time. Nobody hurries here. It's probably this tranquility that's reflected in the prices.

The server brings me to the door and whispers: "We're here. Do you need anything else?"

"No, thank you."

He nods and leaves.

I look at my watch. Four minutes and fifty-three seconds left. Which I now get to spend standing around here...

Chapter 28

Alexander

A few hours earlier...

With a stone-cold expression, I look at Simon, who gazes at me inquisitively. "Nothing?"

"Absolutely nothing," he answers.

I lean back in my chair while he continues spreading out his documents. We're in my living room, and the hacker I hired is reporting that he found nothing incriminating on London.

"I searched through her emails, monitored her phones, looked at all the websites she visited and..." He glances at his business partner Justin, who nods briefly. "...Justin followed her."

"She always went straight home or shopping. No suspicious meetings. Nothing."

"She had the entire weekend before to meet with someone," I speculate.

"True. But she would have had to make contact. I traced her data back three months, then extended it to six, just to be thorough. Nothing."

I lean forward and examine the printouts. Chat logs, website visits. "Not even an attempt to find someone who could use the data?"

"No. She searched for recipes and..." Simon hesitates before tapping on a stack of paper. "Well. Men."

"Men?"

"Forum posts about men acting strangely after one-night stands. She registered and asked questions. She was more concerned with trying to understand some guy named A., cooking, and searching for music, movies, and good books."

I take the forum pages and skim the first few lines.

Yep. She's talking about me. *Heartbreak. My boss. What should I do?*

"Okay, what about traces of the software?"

"Nothing there either. Whoever has this USB hasn't done anything with it yet. It hasn't been offered on the dark web, nor have any parts of the code been uploaded."

"I didn't expect that." I lean back again. "Keep watching her. Maybe she wants to let the matter cool off—or maybe she's waiting for the right moment to blackmail me."

"Okay."

The two of them will have work to do for a while longer. I never wanted to resort to such measures, but I had no other choice.

After the two young guys leave, I find myself confronted with a pile of printed pages.

Messages to her best friend about trivial stuff and a few texts with her parents. I skim only briefly—it feels wrong to pry.

What if I'm wrong about her?

I take the forum pages and read the post she wrote more carefully. In it, she writes quite precisely how she fell in love with her boss, but he broke her heart. She doesn't understand what happened or what she might have done wrong. The encouragement from other forum participants is substantial, but there are also accusations that one shouldn't get involved with one's boss.

I lose myself in the messages and also read her responses, that she doesn't know what to do now, even considering quitting so she doesn't have to see me anymore.

I go to the kitchen, make myself some tea, and start pondering. On my phone, new pictures of Stephanie pop up showing her at the pool in her house with the comment: "One last time in a bikini before the belly starts growing."

I put the phone down again and keep brooding. Maybe I really am wrong about London. But then, who stole the drive?

I'm the only one who knows the safe's combination. Not even my father knows it. And London did have the PIN for my phone to delete the photo, but the safe combination is completely different.

On the one hand, her behavior seems suspicious. On the other, there's always a reasonable explanation.

I *know* I still had the USB with the data. No one else entered my office. Just her and Marc. There was no cleaning staff, no other employees.

No—I push away the thought that it could have been Marc. That makes even less sense.

After all, he wants to take my place so I can return to the States. We've known each other for a good twenty years.

No. It must have been London. Perhaps by accident, or she planned it all along to frame Marc.

Maybe she really wants to blackmail me and get her permanent contract that way. Or she'll pretend she "found" the stick in the trash, hoping I'll be so grateful that I reward her with the position.

It's late. I should get going now. I check my phone once more and read the message that Matthias Volt sent me.

Soon enough, I'll see how London reacts when I'm there for the conversation.

An hour later, I arrive at the restaurant and am escorted to a private room by a staff member. Matthias is already waiting for me and raises his whiskey glass in a toast before standing to shake my hand. The employee leaves us so that we can talk in private.

"Thirsty?"

"Of course."

We sit down next to each other, and he pours me a drink so we can toast.

"Are you really not going to hire her?" I ask, glancing at my watch. 8:51. She's due in nine minutes.

"No. I see a man who's lost his heart but won't admit it yet. I won't interfere."

"Why are you really helping me?"

"It's always good to make connections, maintain them, and build on them. You never know when you might need help. I'll scratch your back, you scratch mine..." He leans in closer to me: "And let's be honest. You only came here today because you're worried about her."

"Nonsense."

"You're looking out for her. Not because you think she'd actually work for me, but because you're afraid I might take her home tonight."

"Think what you like. I'm only here to test how serious she is." He's not entirely wrong, but I'm certainly not going to confirm his suspicion. Especially not while he's sitting there with a grinning broadly, raising his glass to me again.

"We could make a bet. What do you think her reaction will be? Will she sit down and coldly conduct the conversation with me while ignoring you? Or will she leave as soon as she sees you?"

"London is tough. She'll stay."

"Yes, I think so too."

"Then I guess there won't be a bet," I say, taking a sip.

"Then the only question is who she'll choose in the end. You or me?" If only I knew.

"She'll choose you," I say.

"And I believe she'll stay with you," he replies. "What are we betting on?"

"I don't believe in betting money."

"Then let's bet on her," Matthias suggests suddenly. Apparently, he's not acting purely out of the goodness of his heart—he seems energized by the thought of taking the woman away from me.

"If she chooses you, you can have her. Is that what you mean?" I ask.

"That's what I had in mind. So?" He brings his glass closer to mine, and we clink.

Alright, London. It's up to you. If you want to work for him, you belong to him—and I certainly won't interfere or chase after a woman I've known for barely a month.

Women like her are a dime a dozen.

She's just one of many.

And nothing more.

Chapter 29

London

Ten. Just ten seconds to go. I inhale deeply, raise my hand to knock, and fix my eyes on my watch.

Five.

My future is about to be decided. More money. A new boss. Different colleagues.

Three.

A fresh start.

Two.

A second chance.

One.

I knock.

Silence. It's so quiet that I panic for a moment, wondering if I've got the wrong door. Then it opens.

A tall man stands there in a dark blue suit, his tie perfectly in place. His smile is cold, and it makes me take half a step back. He comes across as threatening, and his smile doesn't make it any better. Attractive? Absolutely. But he doesn't seem at all likable.

"Miss Waverley. Punctual. To the second. You haven't been waiting out here, have you?"

"You caught me," I admit, taking his outstretched hand. His grip is firm, commanding. His gaze fixes me and he tugs me forward, forcing me to close the half step I'd taken back.

"Please. Come in."

He releases me, giving me an obvious one-over. "Exquisite taste. I didn't expect you to dress like this."

He seems pleased.

"I rarely wear things like this," I confess, a little embarrassed.

"A woman like you should never wear anything else." His words flatter me more than I'd like to admit. I'm not used to so many compliments.

He steps aside, letting me pass, but as soon as I do, the ground shifts beneath me.

I thought we'd be alone.

Alexander is here.

I freeze in the doorway and while the door is still open and is a perfect escape, I can't move.

"I asked a good friend to join us tonight. We had a few things to discuss, and since he also has a PA, I thought he'd be able to ask the right questions." Mr. Volt shuts the door, his hand settling lightly on my back as he gestures toward a chair opposite Alexander. "Please, sit. Oh, and I'd prefer it if we were on a first-name basis. Just call me Matthias."

Completely overwhelmed, I manage only a curt nod. "Yes. Gladly."

Alex just sits there, his face unreadable, observing me. Matthias sits beside him. I hesitate, still standing. No sense pretending I don't know what this is. So, I'm simply honest and force a scrap of courage to the surface.

"So, you two know each other?"

My résumé did list Alex—there's no way Matthias missed that.

"Not for very long," Matthias says. Alex doesn't say a word.

"Well, then I probably don't need to explain why I'd like to change my workplace," Now more than ever, I need to stand my ground.

I adjust the chair back—the bottom of my dress is voluminous, and I need the space—then sit, lift the whiskey glass, and hold it out to Matthias. "I could use a little of that too."

He smiles, pours, and I wait until he clinks glasses with me before I drink. Alex, on the other hand, just keeps observing me.

"So? What questions do you have for me?" I ask, taking a few sips.

"Are you always this confident?" Matthias asks, looking amused.

"Yes."

"How do you feel about overtime?"

"Reluctant—but sometimes it's unavoidable."

"Working weekends?"

"If it's well-paid, yes."

"Trips abroad?"

"I'm happy to go."

"Fear of flying?"

"No."

"Besides your native language, you speak Spanish and Italian. Basic Portuguese. How come?"

"I learned Spanish in school. Italian from a close friend whose parents barely spoke English. And after one trip to Portugal, where Spanish and English weren't enough, I wanted to be prepared for next time."

"Why not French?"

"I don't like the language."

"Would you learn it to work with me more effectively?"

"If it's part of the job, yes."

"I'd want my PA to live near me. I have a big house with a separate living unit. Would you be willing to move in?"

I hesitate. "Since work shouldn't affect private life: no. Not for all the money in the world."

"And if I doubled your salary?" He's clearly testing me.

"This isn't about money. I love my freedom. I need a private life."

"And if it were only for five years? And in the end, I paid you ten million pounds?" He's testing me really hard. "Then you'd never need to work again, living a comfortable life."

"Money isn't everything."

"Allergies?" His questions fire faster now, barely giving me time to think. A tactic surely. Probably he'll soon ask a question for which he really wants an honest answer. I can't fall for it!

"None. You?"

"None either."

"Good."

"Do you want children?"

"That question isn't permitted and crosses my boundaries."

I try to Alexander's presence.

"Do your parents support you?"

"Yes."

"And your brothers?"

So, he knows about them, even though I haven't mentioned them anywhere. Someone must have been checking my online profiles.

"They do too."

"Are you in love with Alex?"

"Yes."

"Since when?"

Wait!

I hesitate while he laughs, amused, and Alex frowns.

What a mess. And I'd just been thinking that a question might come up that could get me into trouble!

My cheeks flare and I sit there with my mouth open, which only makes him grin more broadly.

"Interesting."

"It's not... it..." I stammer. No, there's no way out of this.

Such a damn mess!

"You've got the job," he suddenly announces, much to Alexander's and my surprise. Matthias nods to me and says: "Your references are enough for me. And I like you. You can start with me on Monday the week after next."

My probation ends on Friday. It would be a perfect transition.

I look at Alex, who should really say something now. But he remains silent.

"I would be very pleased," I murmur, embarrassed.

He's not saying anything even now. So, he's really letting me go? Just like that? Fuck, it hurts infinitely that he's ignoring me like this. I look away dejectedly, then take a deep breath and look back at Matthias.

To hell with it.

"Or you sign with me," Alexander finally says. I look at him hopefully. "You'll get your permanent contract on Monday."

"I'll pay you two thousand more than your old job," Matthias offers me.

"Make your decision," Alexander demands, looking at me grimly. Matthias just smiles.

The stupid thing is that my heart and my mind are telling me two completely different things. My heart says I should stay with Alexander, even if he doesn't love me, but my mind says I have to leave.

"I choose Matthias." I look at him, stand up and offer my hand. "I'll come to your office on Monday after my regular work and sign the contract."

Alexander doesn't flinch while Matthias stands up and takes my hand.

"That was the best choice you could have made, London." He lets go and puts his phone in his pocket. "However, I have to decline."

What?

Alexander isn't the only one looking confused.

"But..." I'm still standing there, not knowing what to do now.

"I've already eaten. If you want to order something, it's on me. I'll leave you two alone. You certainly have a lot to discuss." He nods politely to both of us and then leaves.

I expected many things, but certainly not this. I stare at the roughly plastered wall, the green plants and the Greek ambiance. The vaulted ceiling makes the room seem enormous. There's no window, but there is a statue modeled after the Venus de Milo.

I swallow nervously and sit down again.

What now?

Just a moment later, there's a knock at the door. Alexander calls the person to come in. It's an older server. She asks us what we would like and brings us the menus.

"I'll have water, please. Sparkling, with ice and a slice of lemon," I say and look at Alexander.

"Green tea."

The lady leaves us alone again and closes the door behind her while I open the menu. I simply don't know what to do, so I fidget with it. Alexander, on the other hand, doesn't move, which I can see very well from the corner of my eye.

"You really want to eat now?" he asks me. He sounds angry.

"I last ate at noon today, so yes."

I need to think. Calmly. That's hard to do when he's staring at me the whole time!

"You've made your choice," Alexander says then, without taking his eyes off me.

"My contract expires in a week, and you haven't even had a conversation with me about how things should proceed," I tell him reproachfully.

"I would have. Next week."

"Besides, it's not a good idea for us to keep working together. Too much has happened."

"It's working fine. Isn't it?"

That's enough.

"You're having an affair with Stephanie. Your best friend's wife! She's married!"

"What?" Alexander looks completely surprised.

"I've suspected it for a long time, but now she's there at lunch everyday and..."

"She's pregnant."

"You got her pregnant?" I snap at him angrily.

"It's Marc's. She's just my best friend and yes, she's really clingy right now, but there's nothing between us. There never was anything and there never will be."

And just like that, the wind is taken out of my sails.

"That's why you wanted to leave?"

"Things are strange between us. Your behavior hurt me. So yes. I wanted to leave because I can't stand it anymore. I thought you wanted to hire her as your new PA and..."

"Nonsense. She doesn't even have your qualifications."

That should flatter me now, but I'm far too upset about it.

There's another knock at the door and the server brings the tea and water. "Have you decided on an appetizer yet?"

"Not yet. Please give us a few more minutes." Alexander nods to the server, who immediately leaves again. Her interruption has lightened the situation briefly.

"Why are you acting so strange with me then?" I ask him directly.

"You know why, and I'm no longer willing to pretend I don't know about it."

What on earth is he talking about?

"Because I have feelings for you? Yeah, okay. That's true. You showed me the starry sky, and we slept together three times. It just happened. I can't turn them off!"

I'm getting louder than I intended, Alex, on the other hand, remains calm.

"I meant the other thing."

"Because I applied to Matthias? I had to assume you wouldn't hire me permanently. So, I looked for alternatives. I have bills to pay!"

He doesn't need to know that I have good savings.

"No. You know what I mean. Do I really have to say it?"

I have absolutely no idea what he's talking about.

"Yes! I don't know what you mean."

"You stole my USB."

Excuse me?

"You're angry about a USB?" I ask, confused.

"So, you have it?"

He looks angry and disappointed.

"If I accidentally pocketed one, I'm sorry, but I don't think so. Such a small thing could easily fall down or end up in the trash. I've only carried coffee cups and things from the kitchen in and out of your office."

He's silent staring at me critically.

"Maybe it came along on a tray once, or I accidentally knocked it down. If it's gone, I'm sorry. I... wait. Do you think I deliberately threw it away?"

He keeps not saying anything.

"That's it? You think I threw away a USB drive at some point to annoy you? Are you serious? That's why you're angry?" I'm speechless and need to collect myself briefly. "Was it made of gold, or what?"

Silence.

Absolute silence.

"You swear you didn't take it?"

"Not intentionally. I don't know. I think I would have noticed if I'd taken it to the kitchen. I always sort the dishes right away and put the tray up. If it had been on the tray, it would surely have fallen off and..."

"Okay. That's enough." Alex raises his hand, and I fall silent. "I believe you."

He rubs his temples.

"Do you need a painkiller?"

I open my clutch and dig out my small container with emergency meds: headaches, fever, nausea. Luckily, I always carry these things. "Take it with my water."

"I don't have a headache. I'm just realizing something."

"That I'm not a thief?" I ask bitterly. "I hate being accused when I haven't done anything."

"The only one who could be responsible now is Marc."

Oh.

Oh! Now I get it.

"That USB probably just fell down. Maybe it was vacuumed up when the cleaning staff was here. If they didn't notice, we could check the trash and..."

"No. There was one in my safe. But it was empty."

"Then you deleted the data. Or the drive was damaged!" And then he accuses *me*? "I'm the one who should be angry. Not you!"

"There was data on that drive. Very important data. I had it in my hand and placed it on the table. Marc was there and you came in to bring him a Coke."

I remember that.

"I stepped away briefly to make a phone call. One minute. At most! When I came back, I put the drive in the safe. So, it didn't fall down or get stolen. It was... switched."

I see... Then it must have been Marc. Damn.

"And blaming me made sense to you? Because I was planning to leave, and Marc is your best friend."

"We'd been discussing me going back to the States so he could take my position. Honestly, it doesn't even make sense. Unless..." Alex shakes his head.

"Unless what?"

"It's just a suspicion. But if I put this puzzle piece into the bigger picture—it all fits."

"Fits better than me stealing from you?"

"Unfortunately, yes." Alex takes a deep breath and then takes the menu. "I really should sort this out now, but the evening has been stressful enough."

"If it's so important, do it now." I stand up. "And if you want, I'll come with you."

"I should handle this alone."

"As upset as you are, I'm certainly not letting you go alone."

"I'll call my driver and get you a taxi."

"I said: I'm not letting you go alone." I circle the table. "I'm part of this problem and want to clear my name. If this is why you've been so angry with me these past weeks, maybe I can finally actively do something about it."

Alex stands up and looks at me sternly. "So, you do love me?"

I didn't really want to talk about that right now.

"It's complicated."

"Love is never simple."

"But it should be," I answer sadly.

"Maybe it still can be."

Perhaps.

"You want to go to Marc and Stephanie, I assume?" I ask him.

"Yes."

I take his hand and squeeze it firmly. Confronting his best friend about theft won't be easy for him. "I'm here for you."

Alex lifts my hand, kisses it, and lingers for a moment. I'd like to tell him how angry I am right now, but we'll have time for that later. This comes first.

Chapter 30

Alexander

My father taught me to always listen to my head and never to my heart. The heart only ever longs for what's bad for you. It feels good and right in the moment, but not in the long run. It behaves like lust. After the orgasm, we come back to our senses and only then we see what stupid decisions we made when we couldn't focus. That's the same reason you shouldn't shop when you're hungry.

I believe her. You can immediately tell from London's face whether she's lying or not. Her behavior was clear and logical. She didn't even know the stick had been switched.

But that means it must have been Marc, and I'm slowly beginning to understand what's behind the behavior of both him and Stephanie.

We drive to their place. They live in a huge house her father gave them as a wedding gift. The luxurious property is on the outskirts of London in a *gated community*. My family owns two properties here, so I can get in without any problems.

The driver heads toward their property, which is at the end of the long street.

"Do you have any idea why he did it?" asks London.

We're sitting in the back of the limo, where the driver can neither see nor hear us.

"I have a theory."

"Tell me."

"I don't even want to think about it. But I hope I'm wrong." I glance at her. She seems worried and takes my hand again. I'm not used to this much support from a woman. "You're not angry with me?"

"Oh yes. Very much so. But now isn't the right time." She smiles. It makes me smile back.

"Because I accused you?"

"Among other things."

"Sounds like I should prepare myself for quite a bit."

"Absolutely." She squeezes my hand harder. "But we'll get through this." She seems confident.

We reach the property, and the driver parks. Shortly after he opens the door for us. It's dark outside. Only the streetlights light up the street.

"Wait here. It won't take long," I tell the driver.

He nods and gets back into the car while London and I walk to the front door. I notice that she's getting nervous. I reach for the bell… then pause.

"What if he denies it and blames me?"

"He probably will."

"I'm innocent."

"Yes, I know." I'm certain he did it. Sadly. I just don't know if our friendship will survive this betrayal.

I ring the doorbell. It doesn't take long before Marc opens the door. We could already see him through the small glass windows beside the door.

"Hey, well this is a surprise. What are you two doing here?" He's still smiling. He still seems friendly. I look at my best friend in the eyes and try to stay calm.

"We need to discuss something important. Is Stephanie here too?"

"Um, yes. She's in the home gym, but I'll let her know. Come in first." Marc steps aside and looks at London curiously. "Were you two out?" he asks.

"In a manner of speaking." I force a friendly look.

"Please. This way to the living room."

I'd been here a few times before the wedding, but not after.

We follow Marc and take a seat on the couch while Marc gets his wife.

London and I spend the agonizing moments silently on the couch until Marc returns with Stephanie. At first, she beams when she sees me but then seems startled when she sees London beside me. Her forced smile speaks volumes.

"Hey, you two. Nice surprise."

"We have something important to discuss with you. It couldn't wait," I say and point to the couch across from us. Marc and Stephanie look puzzled but sit down.

"This seems incredibly important," Marc remarks.

"It is. I need to talk to you about something. I have a suspicion, and I have to know what's really going on."

"If this is about our marriage…" Marc stammers.

"Yes, well, our marriage…" Stephanie speaks simultaneously. They look at each other and then back at me. Neither finishes their sentences.

"When you were at my place on Friday, a USB went missing. It contained a copy of the software I've been developing for a long while. Someone switched the drive for a blank one that I put in the safe. And you're the only one who could have done it." I stare at Marc. His expression turns to stone. He even slightly lifts his chin arrogantly, while Stephanie sits quietly next to him without making a sound. She probably knows that Marc stole the drive.

Their reactions are genuine. None of them is surprised or angry. They've just told on themselves.

Shit.

"What makes you think that?" Marc lies laughing nervously. "Why would I do that? Not to mention London was in your office too."

"It couldn't have been her. But yes, I suspected her the whole time."

"How long have you known her? A month?"

"That's right."

"And how long have we known each other? Since we were kids!"

"I know."

"So, you trust a woman you're sleeping with over your best friend?"

Even now, Stephanie doesn't react. This only confirms my theory.

"My best friend wouldn't steal from me. Or let's say… wouldn't make sure I go back to the States, so his marriage doesn't fall apart." Out of the corner of my eye, London's looking at me, confused, while Stephanie stares at the floor with a bright red face. Marc glares at me.

Bull's eye.

"I'm here for the truth," I say coldly. "And this season of "The Mole" ends today."

"Do you think I'm stupid enough to take something from you when I want your position? You agreed to leave. What does this have to do with our marriage?" So, he wants to keep playing this game. I see.

"For a long time, I didn't understand what was really going on here. I thought it was coincidences, or that I was just imagining certain things, but it all makes sense when you put the individual pieces together. The puzzle is complete." I sigh quietly, because I never wanted to say it out loud: "Stephanie is in love with me."

As soon as I say this, she closes her eyes and looks slightly away. Marc sits like a statue. London, however, gasps.

It's out in the open.

The truth needs to come out.

Things have been festering in the dark for far too long.

Chapter 31

London

I'm shaking all over.

Marc glares at Alexander, while Stephanie sits, hands folded, eyes closed.

"I even think you've been in love with me for years. That's why you've always rejected Marc."

"But they got married," I whisper, confused.

"Yes," Stephanie breathes.

When she responds, Marc looks away. He's full of rage and both his hands clench into fists.

"Of course I'm in love with you," Stephanie says, tears rolling down her cheeks. "You're only realizing this now?"

She looks at Alex disdainfully. Marc doesn't comment on any of it, though I can clearly see how much it hurts him. I think I'm slowly beginning to understand what's going on here.

"And then you marry my best friend?" Alex sounds accusatory.

No wonder.

"Because you were supposed to stop the wedding! Instead, you help plan it and you're happy for him!" Stephanie leaps to her feet.

"You pretended to return his feelings, marry him, even got pregnant! Just to make me jealous?" Alex finishes angrily. "How could you do this to him?" Alex leaps up too. "He has sincerely loved you from the beginning, and you're just pretending?"

"I had to find some way to bring you back to England! You would never have returned on your own!"

"I was planning to fly back after the wedding," he responds heatedly.

"That's why I talked to your father."

So, is Stephanie even admitting to manipulating his father?

"You put that idea in his head?"

"I needed you here! To realize you'd lose me if you didn't stop the wedding!" she screams at him desperately. Tearfully, she glances at me and sobs: "When London burst into the church, it was a blessing! I thought it was a sign from heaven. Everything could have all worked out perfectly, but then you ran after her and pushed me back into Marc's arms. What was I supposed to do? Even pretending jealousy over his supposed 'affair' didn't stop the marriage!"

"So that's why you were always asking me about Alex. You were jealous of me," I realize.

"And you said you weren't into him, but you still let him fuck you!" she hisses at me.

Wow. So, her interest in me was just an act too. Vanessa's feeling was right...

But this isn't really about me, it's about Marc and Alex.

"Tell me honestly: Are you even pregnant?" Alex asks her.

"No, she's not," Marc answers for her. "But she was going to pretend she lost the baby so she could cry on your shoulder."

"That's not true!" she snaps.

"You would have tried to sleep with Alex to get him to impregnate you. That way you would have had a reason to get close to him, and eventually he would have fallen in love with you. Out of necessity," Marc blurts out angrily, then glances at Alex guiltily. "That's why I wanted you to leave."

"So, you switched the USB so that..." Alex begins, but Marc immediately interrupts him.

I'm sick to my stomach.

"So, you would suspect her and fire her. Then you wouldn't have had a reason to stay anymore. Back in the US, you would have been far away. Far enough to..." Marc trails off, glancing desperately at Stephanie.

"Oh, come on, I would never have fallen in love with you!"

So that was a plan too.

Marc wanted Alex to leave so Stephanie would have no chance of Alex falling in love with her. The distance would have been too great. He probably hoped that she'd eventually forget about Alex and give him an honest chance. She could have followed him to the States, but she didn't consider that option. I wonder why...

"Why didn't you fly to the States?" I ask her, but Stephanie just huffs indignantly, clicks her tongue, and turns away.

""She wouldn't have gotten a green card. She has a criminal record. No matter how much money you have, the US rejects you immediately. No chance," Marc reveals.

"Criminal record?" I probe.

"Drug use. It was a long time ago," Stephanie defends herself.

"You're my best friend; you could have talked to me anytime. I would have always been there for you!" Alex addresses Marc directly.

"Talk to the man my wife is in love with? You were the root of my problems!" he retorts furiously.

I step between them, even though a table separates them. I raise both arms.

"Okay. Calm down. We have a lot of broken hearts and a whole lot of anger on all sides here. Shouting at each other won't accomplish anything. What we need is a solution—and some distance." Otherwise, this will go on all night.

"What did you do with the drive?" Alex asks.

"Nothing. You were just supposed to throw her out and go back to the States."

"Give it to me. Now," Alex demands.

Marc hesitates for a moment and then walks away, while Alex turns to Stephanie. "And you. I don't even know what to say to you." He struggles for words. "What you did to my best friend, only he can forgive. And the only thing I can tell you is that I'm sorry."

Stephanie looks up at him tearfully.

"I'm sorry that I didn't notice it all these years, otherwise I would have told you much sooner that we're just friends. Nothing more."

"Why her and not me?" she sobs desperately.

"I don't know. I just follow my heart. And it tells me I have feelings for her, not for you."

Okay, wow. I wasn't even aware of that yet... Of course, I'd rather have heard this from him in private but today has been pure chaos anyway.

Stephanie runs out of the living room in tears, leaving Alex and me alone for now. However, we don't even get three seconds before Marc returns and hands Alex the USB. He takes it silently.

"You could have talked to me," Alex says.

It sounds like a peace offering.

"It wouldn't have changed anything."

"You can still talk to me. Anytime. Just not today."

Yep, that's an olive branch.

Even though Marc tried to blame me, I get it. No one deserves to have their feelings played with like that. No one.

Alexander and I leave their house without another word. He opens the limo door for me, waits until I slide inside, then climbs in beside me and closes it.

He presses the intercom to speak to the driver: "Before we go home, we're going to London's."

"London?"

"Um, yes, London's place."

I lean forward and give the driver my address. It's easy to get confused. The driver starts the car, and I shift a little closer to Alex so I can cuddle up to him. No matter what I say now, it wouldn't make the situation any better, but I can be there for him. Stand by him. We've probably left bad times behind. Now it's time to enjoy the good ones.

We go up in my apartment, and I ask, "Would you unzip me?" I could do it myself, but I know how much men appreciate feeling needed. These little gestures are needed to make him feel good. Whether it's opening a jar or unzipping a dress—ultimately it doesn't matter.

Alex approaches me and slowly slides it down so that I can slip the dress off my body. Standing there in just my panties and gold jewelry, I drape the dress over my arm and say, "Thank you. I'll be right back." He doesn't even look at my bare breasts, he's so lost in thought.

"I'm just going to put on something comfortable."

But I don't get far. He grabs me from behind, wraps his arms around me, and nestles his lips against my neck. "Or you stay here with me. I just want to hold you for a moment."

"Okay."

I close my eyes, let the dress fall, and place both hands on his arms. It feels so good to feel him and know he's with me.

"It made sense that it would be you. You wanted my PIN..."

"To unlock your phone."

"You applied to other jobs."

"Because I thought you were having an affair with Stephanie."

"At the boxing club, I didn't mean to embarrass you, just show everyone you were with me."

"Maybe we should have talked to each other."

"We should have."

But being silent together is also quite nice.

Eventually, Alex lets go of me. I go to the bedroom and put on something comfortable.

I'm supposed to pack for a few days so I can spend the weekend with him, so I have to cancel on Vanessa. She's happy for me, though, and can hardly wait to hear all the dirty details that will unfold over the weekend.

It's 4:02 in the morning. After some of my neighbors complained about the noise, we took a limo to his place. As soon as I packed my bag, we couldn't keep our hands off each other in my living room. I enjoyed it. So did he. The neighbors, however, didn't.

We're lying in his bed enjoying our time alone. Even so, it still feels a little strange after the exhausting weeks behind us.

"How could I not notice?" he asks me, though he's staring at the ceiling. Perhaps he just spoke the question aloud because he wanted it out of his head.

"Because she never said anything. Because you'd known each other forever. Because she got married. How could you have possibly guessed? You've known her forever. I think people just block out certain things."

"You suspected it..." He looks at me.

I sit up and tie my hair back.

"I found her behavior suspicious. When she was alone with me, she probably couldn't pretend as well." I want to be honest: "I feel sorry for her. For Marc too, of course. It's a terrible situation for both of them."

"I'm frustrated at both of them," he growls, briefly closing his eyes.

"Stephanie was desperately in love—and unfortunately Marc was too. She should never have married him. She hurt him terribly. But the fact that he tried to pin the theft on me is also pretty extreme."

If Alex had fired me, he would have certainly gone back to the States.

"The team is staying in America. They won't be moving here," Alex decides, which surprises me greatly.

"I'll commute for now and find someone to represent me there. But I'm staying here to take care of the company."

"You're just deciding that spontaneously?" I ask.

"Yes." Alex reaches out to me and brushes my neck. He gently pulls me to his bare chest, kisses me deeply and then wraps both arms around me. "I've fallen in love with London."

"With London?" I ask, examining his warm smile.

"With the city. It's beautiful here. I'm going to stay."

"Oh really? Why?"

"You're here. That's enough."

"You're staying because of me?"

"Would you come with me to the States?"

"Well..." I hesitate. "This is my home. My friends are here. My family. Vanessa, who's like a sister to me."

"If I left, this thing between us couldn't work."

"So, you want to give it a try?"

?" Without even asking what I want? But my smile probably gives me away.

"A woman like you comes along only once in a lifetime." He kisses my forehead. "You said you like flying, right? For the first few weeks and months I'll be traveling a lot. Will you come with me?"

"Of course. If you pay me well."

"I see..." He laughs. "I'll pay you with sex."

"Actually, I'd prefer money."

"Excuse me?" he asks in mock outrage.

"Just kidding." I kiss him softly. "I think it's good that you're not bringing the team here. If you can find someone to lead it on-site, that would be perfect. But don't rush the decision."

"Marc would be perfect for the position. He's doing something similar with his start-up."

Hmm, an idea comes to mind: "So, if things smooth over between you two, couldn't you migrate his company and send him to the States?"

"And trust him with my passion project?" Alex doesn't sound thrilled.

"I know. Stupid idea." It was just a thought.

"It's not stupid. But it's much too soon. I need to process all of today first. Being betrayed like that is quite heavy and it will take time before I can trust him again. Or if I even want to."

"It's late. Or early, depending on how you look at it. The day was long. Don't make any decisions now that you might regret later."

"I'll never regret choosing you." Alex pulls the blanket over our naked bodies and then turns off the light.

"Okay, I can agree with that." I make myself comfortable at his side.

Maybe all of this had to happen so we could have a chance. If things had gone differently, I'd probably be taking another job and never see him again. This way, we both have the chance to build something from our love. Whatever the future brings, I'm ready to find out.

Sign up for my newsletter and receive the bonus chapter for this book:
http://www.luvlee.us/adora-prince-en

Thank you

Thank you so much for buying and reading my book — I truly hope you enjoyed it!
If you did, it would mean the world to me if you could leave a review on Amazon.

With love,
Adora

Printed in Dunstable, United Kingdom

78171655R00107